The G

Captain Joshua Price—commanding officer, undercover operative, anthropologist. He didn't always like what the Galactic MI team had to do to find the answers his superiors wanted—but he knew how to get them . . . no matter what the cost.

Lt. Emma Coollege—call her "Jackknife." Resourceful, fearless, a born survivor. She's the team's on-the-spot expert at everything from weapons to disguises. She's willing to break every rule in the book to get the job done—and she *always* gets the job done.

Master Sgt. Wallace ("Rocky") Stone—tough and deadly, a career soldier. He volunteered for a combat unit so he could be where the action was. But when he found out about Galactic MI, he switched—to get into the *real* action.

Soldiers, scientists, high-tech spies: the Galactic MI agents put their lives on the line for Earth—on alien worlds where death awaits the unwary!

Don't miss the first *GALACTIC MI* adventure—available from Ace Books.

Ace Books by Kevin Randle

The Jefferson's War Series

THE GALACTIC SILVER STAR
THE PRICE OF COMMAND
THE LOST COLONY
THE JANUARY PLATOON
DEATH OF A REGIMENT
CHAIN OF COMMAND

The Star Precinct Series (with Richard Driscoll)

STAR PRECINCT
MIND SLAYER
INSIDE JOB

The Galactic MI Series

GALACTIC MI
THE RAT TRAP

GALACTIC MI
THE RAT TRAP

KEVIN RANDLE

ACE BOOKS, NEW YORK

This book is an Ace original edition,
and has never been previously published.

THE RAT TRAP

An Ace Book/published by arrangement with
the author

PRINTING HISTORY
Ace edition/November 1993

ISBN: 0-441-27243-6

ACE ®
Ace Books are published by The Berkley Publishing Group,
200 Madison Avenue, New York, NY 10016.
ACE and the "A" design
are trademarks belonging to Charter Communications, Inc.

10 9 8 7 6 5 4 3 2 1

CHAPTER 1

Sitting at the console, a half-dozen display screens in front of her, a keyboard near her right hand, and a voice input near her left, Ensign Sara Jane Hunter spotted an object that was so far out that it was nearly invisible to even the most delicate of sensors. Without a word to the Captain or the officer of the deck, Hunter changed the settings and tried to learn more about the thing. All she could tell, given the range, was that it was huge, that it did not fit into the parameters of normal space debris, and that it seemed to be heading, generally, in their direction.

She watched it out of the corner of her eye as she scanned space around them, searching for anything that could get in their way. She noticed clouds of dust, hydrogen ions, bits of matter, two comets that seemed to be so far from any system that it was impossible to tell where they belonged, large bits of rock several hundred meters in diameter, and the other ships of the fleet scattered around the flagship.

The distant object seemed to be paralleling their path, getting no closer to them, and drifting no farther away from them. She increased the magnification, but the routine space debris between them and the object obscured it, making it difficult and sometimes impossible to see.

"Captain, I'm picking something up at the extreme range," she said.

"On the main viewer please."

Hunter touched a button and turned her head, watching as the picture on the main viewer dissolved from the fleet and changed slowly into bands of color and then swirled around, coalescing into a view of space. "On the screen," she said.

"What is it?" asked the Captain.

"Unknown, sir."

"Increase magnification."

"This is as good as it gets," said Hunter. "It's right at our range limits and there is a lot of junk between it and us so I can't tell you much about it."

"Hell," said the navigator, "that's just an asteroid that strayed from a planetary system. There's nothing for us to worry about."

"Ensign?"

"Could be right, Captain. Preliminary figures show that it's about a mile or maybe a little more than that in diameter. I can detect no radiation, visual, heat, or radio coming from it. I have found no indications of a propulsion system at the moment. It seems to be just a big cold chunk of rock drifting through space."

"Is it going to be a hazard to navigation?" asked the Captain.

"No, sir," said the navigator, now standing so that he could see the main viewer. "Too large. You'd have to be flying completely blind and stupid not to see it a long way off. Hell, you could almost fly up on it and still have time to avoid it. Gravitational field would be negligible."

"Okay," said the Captain. "Make note of it, complete with current location and direction of flight."

"Yes, sir," said Hunter.

"Let's return the main viewer to the fleet and our course," ordered the Captain.

"Aye aye, sir."

Hunter turned to the right and put her hands on the keyboard. Staring up at the top of the bulkhead, she thought for a moment and then began to type quickly. SOP called for the use of the keyboard whenever possible. If everyone was using the voice input, the bridge quickly became a babble of unrelated conversations and no one would be able concentrate on anything.

Hunter logged the information into the computer quickly, made another routine scan of the object, and let the computer compare that to its main data base before adding it. Satisfied that she had completed her assignment, she logged off the computer and turned her attention to the sensor displays in front of her.

"Captain, have we changed course?"

"Negative. We have been flying straight and true for the last several hours."

"That asteroid seems to be closer to us now," said Hunter.

"Please put it back on the main viewer," again ordered the Captain.

Hunter touched the buttons and then turned in her chair, seeing if the asteroid looked any different now. It was still partially hidden behind the space debris.

"Navigation?"

"It is on a looping course, and appears now that it will cross the path of the fleet."

The Captain turned and touched a button on the arm of his chair. He leaned forward and said, "*Lexington, Lexington,* this is *Odessa.*"

"*Odessa,* this is *Lexington.*"

"We are tracking an object about a mile in diameter that appears to be on an intersect course with us. It does not seem to be under intelligent control."

There was an instant's hesitation and then, "You are cleared to break formation and investigate and destroy if you believe it necessary."

"Roger. Investigate and destroy."

The Captain said, "Nav, give me a quick course to the asteroid. Targeting, have you been monitoring these conversations."

"Targeting, aye. We have the object in sight and are prepared to fire on it."

"Stand by," said the Captain.

"Aye, sir."

"Can't we get a better look at that thing?" asked the Captain.

Hunter turned to her sensors, worked at it. "New picture coming up, Captain."

"Is it giving off light?"

"Negative, Captain. It has an albedo that is incredible. It reflects nearly all the light hitting it."

"That natural?"

"I don't know," said the navigator.

"I want the science officer up here," said the Captain.

"Aye, sir."

"Ensign Hunter, what can you tell me?"

"Nothing new, Captain. The object has maintained its speed but it seems to have altered its course."

Elisabeth Sladen stepped onto the bridge and said, "You wanted me, Captain?"

"Get with Ensign Hunter, have her brief you and then tell me what you can about that thing out there. I want a report immediately."

"Aye aye, sir."

Hunter punched up everything she had on the asteroid as Sladen leaned over her shoulder. "There it is. Seems to have been attracted to our fleet."

"You sure that it altered its course toward us?"

"Of course not," said Hunter. "I don't have enough data on it to make that assumption. I just noticed that it was getting closer to us and it had seemed to be paralleling our course prior to that."

Sladen reached past Hunter and typed her own questions

into the computer. She straightened up and said, "It seems to have altered course once we made a sensor scan of it."

"Reacting to our scans?"

"Don't know, Captain. We know that some natural phenomena are attracted to energy sources. Magnetic fields attract metals. Might be nothing more than that, though our scans are fairly weak."

"Recommendations?"

"Let it go," said Sladen. "I make it nothing more than a rock."

"Hazard to navigation, Captain," said the navigator. "Destroy it."

"Captain, targeting. My boys and girls could use the practice."

"Any reason not to fire on it?" asked the Captain.

Sladen pushed on Hunter's shoulder, shoving her to the right and out of her chair. Sladen sat down, pulled the keyboard around to where she was comfortable with it, and began to type. A list of data began to parade across the screen, telling her what they knew about the asteroid.

"It's just a rock, Captain," said Sladen. "No reason to shoot it."

"And no reason not. Targeting, you may fire a brace of missiles when ready."

"Targeting, aye."

"I want this on the main viewer," said the Captain. "Full magnification."

Hunter stepped to the right so that she was now standing between the Captain and Sladen with a full view of the screen. She watched as the scene shifted, the magnification increasing. The distant object looked like a misshapen ball, lopsided but almost round.

"Bridge, missiles away."

"Bridge, aye."

The missiles appeared on the screen in the lower left corner as bright points of flame. They streaked upward, toward the asteroid.

"Two minutes to impact," said a voice.

Sladen glanced at one of the small display screens and then asked, "Are you recording?"

"No," said Hunter.

Sladen started the cameras and said, "You should have been recording from the moment you saw something unusual. Intelligence is going to want a complete record of this for review later."

"Couldn't see anything."

"You can't but computer enhancement might be able to tell us something."

"One minute."

The missiles had all but disappeared, the flame from the rear nearly invisible because of the distance. But the missiles were flying true.

"Thirty seconds."

No one saw the blue-tinted wave that radiated from the asteroid at first. It wasn't until the recordings that Sladen made were reviewed that anyone spotted it. The wave expanded outward much like the rings on a pond after a stone had been tossed into it.

The missiles stopped moving as the blue mist touched them and then they exploded, detonating far short of the target. They vanished in a brilliant flash of fire.

The Captain leaned to the right, slammed the button, and snapped, "Targeting."

"Targeting, aye."

"Your missiles failed."

"Yes, sir. we're working on it. Give us a minute."

The Captain spun his chair so that he was facing toward Sladen and Hunter. "You spot anything?"

"No, sir. Missiles just seemed to detonate. We don't know why they did that."

"Lieutenant Sladen?" asked the Captain.

"I saw nothing, sir."

The Captain sat quietly for a moment, staring at the main viewer. Around him the equipment chirped and beeped as it processed the information. There was a rattling from the keyboards as the various staff officers fed additional information into computers, or demanded answers from them.

"Maybe the missiles were defective," said one of the officers.

"Not both of them," snapped the Captain.

"I was only thinking out loud."

"If you can't think straight, keep your mouth shut."

"Aye aye."

Hunter pointed at the screen and said, "I think the object has stopped."

The Captain whirled in his chair and said, "Stopped? Stopped? What do you mean stopped?"

"Just what I said, sir. Stopped. As in it is no longer moving."

"That's impossible," said the navigator.

Hunter waved her hand for silence, or maybe in confusion. "I don't mean stopped in space. I mean it's stopped relative to the fleet. It's maintaining itself at a constant distance from us."

The Captain shook his head. "It could only do that if it was under intelligent control."

CHAPTER
2

The original meeting had been postponed from the night before because of the late arrival of several of the team members. They all met for the first time in the admiral's conference room on board the flagship, the U.S.S. *Lexington*. Like all admirals' conference rooms, it was opulent with thick burgundy carpet on the deck, color-coordinated, high-backed chairs, a highly polished oak table that seemed an extreme expense on a spacecraft, and floor-length drapes in front of the windows that looked out on the blackness of space.

Sara Jane Hunter, because she had spotted the asteroid and was considered the resident expert on it, had taken the chair at the head of the table. Although she was only twenty-five and wore her jet-black hair long, which made her look even younger, she had been put in charge of the meeting for the experience she would gain. She wore her uniform tailored to her trim body, wore the few decorations that she had earned during her military service, and had put on glasses in an attempt to make herself look intellectual. She was worried that no one would accept her as an authority on the subject simply because she looked too young to have graduated from high school, let alone be an officer assigned to the fleet.

She sat quietly, studying the array of buttons on the table in front of her. They controlled the projectors, both slide and holo, the drapes over the windows, and the doors that hid the screen concealed on the bulkhead. She did not look up as the others arrived, afraid of what she'd see. When each of the chairs was filled, she glanced up and said, somewhat self-consciously, "I guess the first order of business is to introduce everyone. I have a list of names here so when I call yours, please raise a hand."

She turned to look at Sladen, the only other person she knew. Letting her gaze slide away, she said, "First is Lieutenant Commander Wallace Stone." Stone raised a hand and grinned broadly. "Next to him is Lieutenant Elisabeth Sladen and then Lieutenant Junior Grade Jo Grant. They are the military flight crew."

Hunter moved a finger down the list and began to read the names more quickly. "We have Dr. Stephen Ellis, a computer expert; Dr. Thomas De Anna, an astronomer; Dr. Henry Barnes, a chemist; Frank Jackson, a geologist; Dr. Emma Coollege, an astrophysicist; and Captain Joshua Price, whose function on this team has been left blank."

Price, a tall, thin man with brown hair and blue eyes, tried to keep from laughing. He let his gaze slide from Hunter to Coollege, who he knew was no doctor and no astrophysicist. Then he glanced at Stone who was masquerading as a lieutenant commander. Stone was a sergeant on his staff and hoped he would remember that.

Finally he said, "I'm not exactly sure why I'm here either, other than I was ordered to be here."

Hunter nodded and turned her attention to the buttons in front of her. She opened the doors in front of the screen, dimmed the lights, and turned on the slide projector. "This seems like an unnecessary burden on us. If the Captain would spin the ship, you could look out on the asteroid from here."

"And not see a damned thing," said Coollege. "Not at the

distance it is holding from the fleet." She was nearly as tall as Price but had chopped her hair short as military regulations dictated, though here no one was supposed to know of her military connections. She had brought a number of charts and tables with her, but she was more familiar with various personal weapons and the use of them.

Hunter shrugged and pointed to the picture. "I suppose that everyone here knows by now that there is no longer any question about the nature of the asteroid. It is, in fact, some kind of space vehicle. Obviously it is not something we built nor is it the popular view of an alien craft."

The slide changed, showing another photo of the asteroid, though it looked almost the same. Hunter said, "It seems to be a large craft meant for interstellar voyages. Our sensors do not suggest there are any biological creatures . . . or, rather, beings on board."

She faced the group. "Since the missiles attempted the destruction of the asteroid, there has been a steady stream of radio signals. They have been broadcast on a wide range of frequencies, sometimes overwhelming the other signals on those specific frequencies and bleeding all over the radio. Dr. Ellis and his crypto people have been working to break the code. Dr. Ellis."

Ellis sat up straighter, surveyed the group, and then glanced at the screen. Ellis was the oldest of the group with a smattering of gray in his brown hair. He was a short, thin, nervous man wearing a jumpsuit in chocolate-brown. He rubbed his chin as if thinking deeply and then simply shook his head. "I'm afraid that the point of the messages has escaped us. We just haven't figured it out. The important point is that the message, whatever it is, repeats itself."

"How do you know?" asked Price.

"We've broken the signal down to its elements and charted them on the computer. After twelve hours, the same set of signals appears in the same order. We're watching and recording in case they suddenly change the signal but to this point they haven't."

Coollege chimed in. "Have you attempted to convert it to dots and dashes and use prime numbers to define the sizes of the rectangle?"

"Dr. Drake, who headed Project Ozma in the 1960s, might have tried that. His idea was simplicity and seemed to make sense, so we did attempt to convert the signal that way, but it has proved useless."

"Well," said Coollege, "why not give it to the crypto boys and girls in intelligence and see if they can think of anything new?"

"Because I wanted to keep this out of the hands of the military," said Ellis.

Hunter snapped her head around and stared at him. "Now what in the hell is that all about? If it wasn't for us, you wouldn't be here and you wouldn't know what we found."

"And your first move was to fire on it."

"Because it seemed to be a hazard to navigation," said Sladen, her voice suddenly angry. "Do you think we'd have shot at it if we had known."

Stone slammed a hand to the tabletop with a sound like a pistol shot. "Knock it off here. This is not the place to begin to argue about who is right and wrong. We have a task to complete together. Dr. Ellis, I think you owe the military an apology because we thought we were firing at a natural object that could have damaged part of the fleet."

Ellis sat glaring at Hunter and then slowly turned so that he was looking right at Stone. Finally he said, "I suppose you are right. Still, we find an alien artifact and the first thing we do is shoot at it."

Stone could see that Hunter was going to protest so he held up his hand. "He understands that we didn't know. Now, Ensign Hunter, apologize for your anger."

"I will not."

"Ensign, that is a lawful order and for the sake of harmony in this adventure, I am going to insist."

Price sat there trying not to laugh. Stone, the old NCO masquerading as a naval officer, was using the same technique to intimidate the ensign that he would have used if he were in his proper uniform as a high-ranking sergeant and speaking to a second lieutenant.

"Aye aye, sir. Dr. Ellis, I am sorry that I responded with anger."

That finished, Sladen asked, "Is there anything else that we know?"

Coollege said, "I have some of the preliminary information run on the asteroid . . . though with the discussion we've already had, I think that it might be a little like old news."

"Go ahead, Doctor," said Hunter.

Coollege fumbled through her report on the structure of the asteroid, or as much of it as she could. She read from the report that had been given to her that morning and stumbled over some of the technical names. She'd been briefed on them, but without them written out phonetically, she mispronounced a few of them. Barnes, the small, hairy chemist, corrected her once and then didn't bother again.

When Coollege finished, Hunter took over the meeting again. "Our flight to the asteroid has been scheduled for this afternoon. Simple reconnaissance before we plan anything else."

"Now wait a minute," said Barnes, interrupting. "Wait a minute. Nobody said a thing about flying over there."

Price couldn't resist it. "You've been flying through space since you got on this ship."

"It's not the same," said Barnes. "I'm not going."

Hunter looked at him and shrugged. "Fine. I never thought a chemist would be of much use anyway."

Again Stone interrupted. "Dr. Barnes, you have been assigned to this crew and you will obey your orders."

"I'm a civilian here, Commander. You have no authority over me."

Stone laughed out loud. "I just don't understand where you get these silly ideas. When you signed on to the ship, you made certain concessions. One of them was to obey the lawful orders of the officers of the fleet. You have been given a lawful order. You will obey it or you will be stripped of your authority here, reduced to the lowest grade, and charged for the food you eat, the air you breathe, and the water you drink."

Barnes sat silently for a moment and then said, "It was just a shock. That's all."

"Ensign Hunter," said Stone.

"This will be a quick exploration. Possibly with an EVA depending on what we see, and then a return here for the planning of a long-term mission. Time in space will be no more than twenty-four hours and probably less than that. Questions?"

"Take-off time?" asked Price.

"Fourteen hundred hours this afternoon. We'll assemble in the shuttle bay at thirteen hundred."

As they left the conference room, Price pushed his way closer to Coollege and said, "Are you going to have some lunch, Doctor?"

She looked at him, her eyes wide and innocent. "Why, Captain, I just don't know."

"Come on, Jackknife, have lunch with me or I'll blow your cover."

"Sir, should you be talking like that where someone might overhear?"

Price looked around but there was no one close and no one listening. He said, "When did this come about?"

"Last night. The Colonel called and asked me up to his conference room. He gave me a package of information to study and told me that I was assigned to this mission."

"He mentioned nothing to me about it."

They walked down the long, narrow corridor. They stopped at the mid-lift and waited for the doors to open. Price said, "I wish he'd gone through the chain of command."

"He's the Colonel."

"Of course."

The door opened and there were three people inside. Price

let Coollege enter first and then turned to face the door. He said nothing to her as they ascended through the center of the ship. When they reached the upper level, everyone exited. Price held back, letting the others hurry ahead.

"The Colonel say anything specific to you?" asked Price.

"He knew that there would be problems planting all of us on this mission."

"So he gave them me to wonder about, but you and Stone seem to have real reasons for being there."

"Yes, sir."

Price felt a twist of anger in his belly. He didn't mind the Colonel calling the shots. Hell, that was his job. He just wished the Colonel had let him know about it before he walked into the briefing.

"He tell you anything that Hunter and her people don't know?"

"No, sir. I think he wants me to head in cold so that my thinking won't be colored by all those other ideas. Get it fresh."

They reached the dining area and saw a short line waiting to get in to get fed. Price looked at the line and shook his head. "I don't want to wait."

Coollege pulled him forward. "Won't be very long."

There was a voice from behind him. Hunter and Sladen were there and Hunter asked, "You two know each other?"

"Not really," said Price, lying. "I have briefed Dr. Coollege's group a number of times."

"Just what do you do?" asked Sladen. Her naval rank of lieutenant was the same as Price's captain. She wasn't intimidated by him.

"I do a lot of things," he said noncommittally.

"Intelligence," said Hunter.

"He's a damned spy," said Sladen.

There was nothing for Price to do but laugh. "Intelligence it is, but not spying. At least not in the classical sense. My task is to merely interview flight crews on their return and to offer them information about what they might be forced to face to complete the follow-on missions. I have certainly engaged in nothing like spying."

"Sure," said Sladen.

"Captain," said Hunter, "maybe it would be better if you didn't accompany us on this."

"Ensign, I'm there as another observer. Is there a problem with space limitations, cargo capacity, or am I taking the place of another officer or scientist who would make a greater contribution to the mission?"

"No, sir."

Sladen asked, "Who do you report to?"

"I am not in your chain of command, nor am I there to judge your performance. I am a militarily qualified observer for this mission."

Sladen lowered her voice and said, "I don't like this. Who has command?"

"Commander Stone on the flight over and you on the asteroid if that makes you happy," said Price. "This is a Navy mission. I'm along as an observer."

"As long as we understand that," said Sladen. She pushed forward to the front of the line and grabbed a tray. There were mumbled protests from those who had been in front of her but no one tried to stop her. Everyone understood that those with a short time to eat were allowed to move to the front of the line. The honor system was used.

Price said to Hunter, "You'd better help her cool down before we hit the shuttle."

"Yes, sir." She hesitated and then hurried forward to join Sladen.

"Well," said Coollege, "maybe the Colonel was right to salt the staff this way."

Price nodded and said, "I just wish he'd briefed me on this. I don't want to fuck up his thinking on it. Looks like the Navy is already up in arms."

"We're all on the same side."

"Which is something the Navy sometimes forgets . . . no, that's not completely fair. We sometimes forget it too. Maybe

you'd better join them for lunch to keep the cover intact. I'll
head back to the office."

"If you think that'll help," she said.

Price turned to go. "Couldn't hurt."

CHAPTER
3

Price stood in front of the small intelligence office on a middle deck of the flagship and waited for it to iris open. He entered and sat down at the main console. It was a wraparound desk with half a dozen screens, a keyboard, and an audio input. He reached over and pulled the keyboard toward him, but couldn't think of a question to ask or what information he wanted. He was caught in the black void between knowing nothing about the mission and not knowing enough to ask a few serious, intelligent questions.

Behind him the door irised again and he turned. "Morning, Colonel."

The Colonel was a small man with black hair, very white skin, and deep brown eyes. He rarely set foot on a planet and hoped to keep it that way. He decided that he liked space, liked the clean environment, and liked the oxygen-rich atmosphere. Planets were dirty, germ-ridden, and the oxygen was not always in abundance.

"I believe you and I need to have a little talk," said the Colonel.

"Yes, sir." Price turned in his chair but violated military courtesy by not standing.

The Colonel dropped into another of the chairs and said, "We don't know a thing about that asteroid. It is under intelligent control or, rather, was constructed by an intelligence. It has been transmitting a signal to us that we have not been able to decode. The answers are over there." He gestured toward the bulkhead and space beyond it.

Price nodded, though he'd just heard all that. "Just what are you looking for, sir?"

"That thing is far beyond our technological capabilities. We couldn't move an asteroid through space. Nor can we shield our ships so effectively from sensor probes. And . . . there is the way they destroyed our missiles."

"What do you mean by them destroying our missiles?" asked Price.

"This is not for publication and I don't want this information to be discussed outside of this room. We've spent the night analyzing the sensor tapes and that asteroid destroyed our missiles. It produced a blue mist that fanned out from it, almost as if it shed an outer skin. The missiles detonated when it touched them."

Price grinned broadly. "I thought we were wasting too much effort on a scientific mission. I couldn't figure out why Rocky was on the shuttle crew, Jackknife was pretending to be a scientist, and I was assigned to this crew without any role at all."

"You give the scientists someone to hate. They won't be looking for another spy."

"I've been trying to discourage the use of that term," said Price, grinning.

The Colonel waved a hand. "Your job is to find out all you can about that defensive system."

"I may not understand it," said Price.

"I'm not worried about that. I want you there, looking, so that we can ask the right questions when the scientists return from their expedition."

"Certainly, Colonel."

The Colonel stood up. "For the duration of the mission,

you don't know either Stone or Coollege."

"That's going to be a little difficult. They've already seen me talking to Coollege."

"You don't know her well. You stay back and you watch what happens. That's all you do. Observe and then report."

"Yes, sir."

The Colonel climbed slowly to his feet, pushing himself up, and said, "I'll expect a full verbal report from you on your return."

"Yes, sir."

The Colonel stepped through the door and disappeared. Price turned back to the console, more confused than ever. Why did the Colonel think that anything found on the asteroid would not be shared with all branches of the military? He wondered if there was something more in his instructions. The Colonel was becoming famous for providing as little information as possible to his officers so that the men and women on the scene would be allowed to operate without fear of restraint or preconceived notions. He began to wonder about the makeup of the exploration team. Maybe there was someone on it that the Colonel didn't trust and that was why he carefully planted his people on all aspects of the team. He had infiltrated the shuttle crew, the scientific staff, and the military staff.

He looked at the chronometer set between two of the screens and saw that it was nearly time to meet the others in the shuttle bay. He stood up, turned off the equipment not being used, and moved toward the hatch.

When Price stepped through the hatch into the shuttle bay, most of the others were already there, wearing their flight suits. Barnes was walking in a tiny circle, staring at the deck, almost as if afraid to look at the shuttle itself.

Stone, looking impressive as a lieutenant commander, was up in the cockpit, hanging out the side window like an airline pilot on Earth.

Hunter, carrying an electronic clipboard, pressed a button

and said, "I didn't think you were going to make it on time, Captain."

"Why not call me Tree? All my friends do."

"I don't plan on becoming a friend of yours," said Hunter, taking her cue from Sladen earlier.

But Sladen was no longer angry now that the question of command was resolved. She pushed forward and said, "Well, I do, Tree. Call me Liz, if you like. Not all of us are assholes as you'll learn soon enough."

"I think someone had better teach your ensign some manners. It'll make life easier for all of us."

"Ignore her. She doesn't have a brain."

Price grinned and said, "Sounds like good advice to me. I will."

A Klaxon sounded and Price looked toward the control bay. Through the glass he could see the Colonel standing there watching the operation. But the Colonel wasn't alone. Half a dozen other senior officers stood behind him, waiting for the shuttle launch.

"Time to board," said Hunter.

Barnes stood flat-footed, staring at the Klaxon as if it were some kind of demon announcing his imminent death. He wiped a hand over his face and rubbed his chest, leaving a ragged stain on his flight suit. He made no move to enter the shuttle, ignoring those around him.

Price stood back and watched the others. Coollege climbed on board quickly, as did most of the scientists. Barnes held back, away from the shuttle, staring at it.

Hunter walked toward him and said, "Come on, Doctor. There's no reason to be concerned."

"I don't like the little ones. I just don't like them at all."

"We don't have time to worry about that," said Hunter. "You're as safe on the shuttle as you are on any of the ships in the fleet. Now, please, Doctor." She took his elbow and guided him toward the hatch.

Sladen lowered her voice and said, "The old goat just wants a little extra attention."

"He's what? The geologist?" Price said.

"Chemist."

"Well, there you have it. Sits around the lab all day and never has to worry about anything but who'll clean his beakers. Now he's got Hunter watching out for him."

"You're saying he's a dirty old man."

"Exactly," said Price.

When the scientists were on board, Hunter turned and motioned at Sladen. "I guess she wants us," she said.

"Well, let's not keep her waiting."

They both boarded the shuttle and dropped into the closest seats. Price reached up, pulled down the shoulder harness, and held it in his left hand as he groped for the lap belt. He buckled the shoulder harness into the buckle, then fastened the two pieces together.

Hunter, in her role as the deputy mission leader, made sure that everyone was properly buckled in, checked the hatch to make sure that it was tightly closed, and then walked up the narrow aisle and took a seat just behind the hatch that led up to the flight deck.

Over the intercom, Stone said, "We are preparing for launch. Outside environment has been drained of air and the outer doors have been opened. This is it, boys and girls."

There was no feeling of motion. Through the small portholes along the fuselage, Price could see the dimmed lights of the shuttle bay. They seemed to be slipping to the rear as the shuttle moved. The huge bay doors were wide open and as they dropped from the bay, into the blackness of space, there was only the slightest change in the interior pressure.

Then there was a push from the rear as the shuttle turned, the nose pointed at the asteroid for a moment. They began to accelerate rapidly, the shuttle aimed at a point where the asteroid would be in fifteen hours.

"We're on the way," said Sladen quietly.

"That we are."

The pushing stopped after three minutes and there was no

longer any indication that they were moving. The fleet was falling away to the rear, but that could have been the fleet rather than the shuttle.

Hunter unbuckled herself and then spun her seat around so that she could look back at the rest of the team. "I understand Dr. De Anna has an update briefing for us."

De Anna nodded and opened one of the pockets on his flight suit, extracting a small notepad. De Anna was a big, stocky man with blond hair and blond eyebrows so fine that they were nearly invisible. He didn't have the blue eyes to go with the blond hair, and his nose was long and massive, seeming to dominate his face.

"We did some preliminary work. While the rest of you were eating." He grinned to show it was a joke. "While you were eating, I was trying to learn something about the age of the asteroid. We've been able to get some interesting radiation readings and by assuming that it is not a natural object, but one that was manufactured completely, we have been able to estimate its age."

"How old?" asked Jackson.

"About fifteen thousand years."

"My God."

"Yes, it is quite amazing, but you must remember the vast distances of space." He stopped, realizing how pompous he sounded. "I guess that you all know that."

"But fifteen thousand years . . . there can't be anything alive on it?" said Ellis.

Hunter took over again. "We can make no assumptions about that. It could be some kind of colony ship, set up for a long voyage."

"But fifteen thousand years."

"How accurate are those readings?" asked Coollege.

"Well, the major problem is that we have very little for comparison and we needed to make a number of assumptions, some of them fairly wild, so I wouldn't be surprised if we were off as much as fifty percent."

"Not very good," said Coollege.

De Anna shrugged and laughed. "It's the best we could do. A horseback guess."

"Anything else?" asked Hunter.

"Not from me. I just worked out an age since there were those back on the ship who wanted to know how long it had been in space."

"Nothing biological on board," said Barnes. "I mean, nothing living."

De Anna turned his attention to the small chemist. "Now I don't know what I said that could lead to that conclusion. I have said nothing that would rule that out. Personally, I don't think it is inhabited, only because of the age of the thing, but that is my own opinion."

"We must be prepared for anything. And there is the possibility of inhabitants," insisted Hunter.

"But we will continue to treat it as if it were an uninhabited asteroid," said Sladen.

Price glanced at her. "Taking over the meeting?"

"No," she whispered. "I just don't want to get bogged down in a lot of trivia."

"That happens a lot when you have so many self-important people around," said Price.

Hunter stood up and moved toward the center of the shuttle. She stepped carefully, almost like a person who'd taken one drink too many. The artificial gravity on the shuttle was only about a tenth of ship normal.

"I think that we should enter a rest mode. There is nothing that we can do for the next several hours. Observations will continue on the ship and if anything is noticed, it'll be relayed to us here."

"This doesn't seem to have been well thought out," said Price. "A rest period in the middle of the afternoon and a scheduled landing at what, four in the morning?"

"We do what we have to," said Sladen.

Price turned his attention to Coollege who was sitting with the scientists trying to look as if she knew what she was doing and trying to look inconspicuous. She wasn't saying a word.

She'd learned long ago the best move was to remain quiet whenever possible.

"We will remain quiet," said Hunter, "resting, until we get the wake-up call from the main ship. Those are the orders. Questions?"

There were none and the lights in the shuttle dimmed until they were little more than a dull red glow.

CHAPTER 4

Price found that he could sleep, even if it was supposed to be the middle of the afternoon or early evening. And when the lights came up early the next morning, he was ready and rested. He pushed himself out of his seat, walked forward, and then looked up into the cockpit of the shuttle.

Stone was sitting in the command pilot's seat, his fingers laced behind his head, staring out into space. He glanced back and said, "Come on up, Captain."

The view through the shuttle's windshield was spectacular. The asteroid filled it, the glow of it making it almost impossible to study its surface. It looked like a giant silver basketball with a little mud stuck to the surface. There were no other protrusions, wings, rings, or obvious hatches. There were no surface details that would provide a clue about the construction techniques.

"Kind of impressive," said Stone.

"How long have you been looking at it?"

"Couple of hours. Hasn't changed much as we got closer. Some detail but that's all."

"You get a briefing from the Colonel?" asked Price quietly.

"You mean the mist?"

"Yeah. We penetrated closer than the missiles?"

"Not yet, Captain. Another couple of thousand kilometers before we get that close."

Price nodded and suddenly wondered if anyone on the *Lexington* had thought about that. And if they had, if they were worried about it.

"They brief you?"

"Suggested that we approach slowly and try to appear as nonhostile as possible. The command staff believes that it was the size and speed of the missiles that triggered the destructive mist."

Price snorted. "Sure but none of them are here. They're all nice and safe on the *Lexington*."

"Yes, sir," said Stone, forgetting for the moment that he now held the superior rank.

"Watch it," cautioned Price.

Hunter stuck her head up and then said, "If you'll return to your seat, Captain Price."

Price was about to protest and then simply nodded. He climbed from the flight deck and walked back to his seat. As he sat down, Sladen asked, "Learn anything?"

"Just saw the asteroid up close."

Hunter pointed to the bulkhead behind her and said, "Nose cameras have been turned on so that we can all watch the approach."

Again the lights were dimmed, but now they could all see the asteroid. The view was nearly as impressive as that from the flight deck. There was no doubt that the asteroid had been built on another planet, that it was an interplanetary craft, and that it was purposefully staying close to the fleet, now that it had discovered it.

While the others leaned forward, trying for a better look, Price was not. Unlike them, he knew of the blue mist and he didn't believe the reasoning of the scientists and intelligence officers on the *Lexington*.

Sladen picked up on his unease and asked, "There something you haven't shared?"

"Landings," said Price, leaning close. "I hate landings. It's the time when crashes take place. I wouldn't mind these shuttle trips if we could figure out a way to get down without landing."

"You can hold my hand if it will make you feel better," said Sladen.

Price thought, for the moment, that she was being sarcastic, and then realized that she wasn't. "No, thanks. I'll be fine in a few minutes."

They were approaching the asteroid slowly now. Very slowly. The scene changed as they closed on it. And the closer they came, the jumpier Price became. He could visualize the blue mist radiating from the asteroid. He wondered if the mist had caused the warheads of the missiles to explode or if there was something in it that would destroy the shuttle. Since they carried no explosives, maybe the blue mist, if launched, would do nothing to them.

Price kept his eyes on the screen, watching for a sign that the mist had been deployed. He searched space around the asteroid, looking for a hint that the situation had changed, wondering if they were all going to die in the next few minutes.

The distance between them and the asteroid was shrinking so slowly that Price couldn't see any difference. He knew that they were nearing it and he felt his stomach begin to flip-flop. The situation was something that he could do nothing about. He could only sit there, hoping that those on the ship, those who had authorized the mission, had been correct in their analysis.

Then, suddenly, Price realized that they were well inside of the range of the blue mist. The scene had changed significantly suddenly, as if there were a delay between real time and what the camera was showing them. The mist hadn't been launched at them. They were already beginning the process of landing on the asteroid. They had made it safely.

From the cockpit came Stone's voice. "We're about half a klick from touchdown. Let's get ready."

They all had their eyes locked on the asteroid now. It was a gigantic silver orb that filled the screen. There was no texture to it. No sign of rivets, seams, or hatches. Just bright, silver, unblemished metal.

There was a whine from the servos as the wheels were extended. A few moments later the shuttle touched down gently, the wheels keeping it from resting on its belly. The approach had been like that of a helicopter to the top of a building on Earth.

Stone leaned back in his seat and exhaled slowly. "We're here," he said over the intercom.

Sladen unbuckled her seat belt and tossed the ends of the strap over the back of her seat. She twisted around, looking for Hunter, and said, "Who gets to lead the first party out?"

"Let's get the preliminaries out of the way."

"What's left to do?" she asked.

"Radiation readings," said Hunter. "We don't want to light up like last year's Christmas tree."

Sladen lowered her voice and said to Price, "She's becoming a real pain in the ass."

"She might be right."

De Anna said, "Our EVA suits have enough shielding to protect us for this. Radiation levels are very low. I've been watching that."

"Great," said Sladen. "I'll get suited up and ready to go."

Hunter looked uncomfortable. "I thought I'd take the first group out."

"The deputy mission commander should remain behind to coordinate," said Sladen.

"I'm going too," said Price.

"Now wait a minute," said Hunter. "I want Jackson and De Anna on the team."

"And me and Sladen," said Price. "The perfect team for the first EVA."

"I'd like to go," said Coollege.

"We have an astronomer on the team," said Price, grinning. "One should stay here to run a few tests and make a few readings."

Hunter said, "He's right. I think the makeup of the first team out is fine."

Stone climbed down from the flight deck and then leaned back, against the bulkhead. "Maybe I should lead this EVA," he said.

"No," said Hunter. "We're going to need you right here. Have you alerted the *Lexington* that we're down on the asteroid's surface?"

"Of course, though they knew it without the need for us to tell them."

De Anna, who had been staring out one of the portholes, turned to the main group. "It's going to be . . . dangerous out there. Little gravity and the surface isn't going to provide solid traction. Looks like it's been pitted by micrometeors. Couple of fist-size craters. The main area of interest is an outcropping of rock about fifty meters from the shuttle. We'll want to take a look at that."

Price, still sitting, said, "You know, that strikes me as a little strange. They create this thing and then leave those bizarre hunks of rock."

"Which is why they are interesting," said De Anna.

"We're wasting time here," said Hunter. "Let's get suited up and ready to go."

Price pushed himself out of the seat and walked to the rear of the shuttle. He opened a locker and began to pull out the pieces of the suit. He sat back, in the closest seat, and began pulling on the bottom of the suit, sticking his feet into the boots, and pulling on the suit like a giant coverall. He stood up, stuck his arms in, and twisted around, pulling it up over his shoulders.

Around him, the others on the EVA team began to climb into their suits. Price sat down again, picked up the helmet, checked it out, worked the visor, and then sat quietly, the helmet in his lap, and waited.

Fifteen minutes later they were grouped around the airlock. Hunter stood there, her back to it, looking as if she wanted to say something important, but there were no words. Finally she turned, opened the airlock, and stepped back, out of the way.

Sladen took the lead. She moved into the interior of the lock. She sat down without a word, checked her helmet, and then put it on, twisting it right, pulling it down until there was a click, and then turning partially to the left.

The other three joined her there. Two of them sat down and Price stood near the rear hatch. As soon as they were all set, Price used the radio in his suit to tell Hunter, "We're ready now."

"Evacuate the air."

"Roger."

As soon as the air was sucked from the airlock, Sladen stood and slammed the palm of her hand into the switch. The hatch irised open, revealing the cold gleaming metal of the asteroid. She centered herself in the hatch and dropped to the surface, slipped and fell on her butt.

"Shit!"

Price laughed and said, "Great first words on an alien artifact."

Sladen still wasn't thinking historically because she said, "Watch that first step, it's tricky."

Hunter came over the radio. "There a problem?"

"Negative. I slipped on exit."

The EVA team assembled on the outside and the hatch irised closed. De Anna, standing to one side, his breathing audible over the radio, said, "The outcropping?"

"Right. Single file. Be careful and remember there is very little gravity associated with this."

They strung out working their way across the asteroid. It was like walking on a sheet of ice but they didn't have gravity to assist them. They had to set a foot down solidly, shift the weight slowly, and then move the trailing foot forward. The tiny craters from micrometeors helped.

They reached the outcropping and stopped. De Anna pointed out an opening in it that looked like the entrance to a cave. The solid, flat metal of the asteroid's surface ran right into the opening looking like a floor.

Sladen flashed a light into it but saw no instruments, wires, antennae, hatches, or anything else that gave a clue about the opening. She turned out the light.

Jackson said, "It might be a natural opening, but I would doubt it. Just a little too convenient."

Sladen felt silly but said, "Cover me."

"Go ahead," said Price.

Over the radio Hunter said, "Hold it. What are you planning on out there?"

"We're going to inspect the outcropping."

"Roger that, but don't go too far in. Keep the radio lines open."

"Roger."

Price took a deep breath and tried to think of a way to stop the mission for a moment. He wanted time to think. He wanted to analyze and evaluate, not plunge on ahead.

Sladen, however, didn't hesitate. She ducked her head, slid a foot forward, and stepped inside. No lights flashed, no buzzers sounded, and no bells rang. She moved deeper, feeling the rocky wall with her gloved fingers. It left a black smear on the material where the rock crumbled.

Ten feet inside, she found a shallow decline that had been impossible to see from the entrance. It twisted to the right out of sight, looking as if it ended.

"De Anna, you want to spot me?" she asked.

"Sure."

"Just inside where you can watch me."

De Anna entered carefully, a hand out to brace himself against the rock of the wall.

"Going down," said Sladen.

The interior didn't change. The corridor was about six feet wide and came to a peak over her head. The floor was the same smooth metal as the outside of the asteroid. She came

to another bend and turned. She could barely see the top of
De Anna's head.

"You'd better bring in Jackson," she said, "and then move
up to this point."

"I understand."

As soon as De Anna started down, Sladen turned the corner
and began to work her way deeper into the asteroid. She
hadn't gone far when the tunnel swung back the other way
and she called for another shift.

Now Price was just inside the outcropping, Jackson was
at the first turn, De Anna at the second, and Sladen was
moving down a long, dark tunnel. She stopped after fifty
meters, looked to the rear, and then continued on.

In the distance she thought that she saw something. Just
a flash of light that vanished in an instant. She wasn't sure
that she'd seen a thing so she didn't mention it.

Hunter listened to the messages as they were relayed one
at a time. She tried to keep track of what was happening but
they had no charts showing the interior of the asterior. All
she could do was guess.

Stone had been sitting in the pilot's seat on the flight deck
watching until Price entered the outcropping. He then made
his way down to the rear cabin.

"What's going on?"

Hunter looked up from the chart she had. "They've found
an entrance that seems to be taking them toward the interi-
or."

The radio crackled and Price said, "We're going to move
up one more place."

Hunter used her radio. "Negative. Pull back for now."

Price relayed the message along and then radioed, "Sladen
is continuing on."

Hunter shouted, "Negative. Negative. Return to the shuttle
now."

She waited and when there was no response, she radioed

them again. Finally she turned to Stone and said, "God damn those idiots anyhow."

Forty-five minutes later she realized that the EVA team was not coming back on its own and that something was going to have to be done in a hurry if they were going to rescue them. The air supply would run out in another hour and a half and after that they could go collect the bodies.

CHAPTER

5

Hunter said that she would lead the second team that would include Coollege, Grant, Ellis, and Barnes. Each would carry spare tanks for those who had been on the first team. Hunter made the decision without consulting either Stone or the main ship, figuring that they would be able to find the first team, resupply their oxygen, and then get the hell out.

Hunter didn't allow any discussion. Now that she had made up her mind, she was in a hurry. She tossed the spare space-suits to the others and grabbed her own. She struggled into it, hurrying as fast as she could. She urged the others to hurry, demanding that they stopped screwing around.

Once in her suit, she put on the helmet and hit the button to recycle the airlock. As soon as the hatch opened, she stepped through and then used the radio. "Let's go, people. Time is wasting."

Coollege entered next but didn't sit down. She waited at the hatch while Stone handed her the spare oxygen tanks. She stacked those to one side. As soon as they were stacked, the others entered.

Hunter hit the switch and the hatch closed. She leapt across the airlock, evacuated the air, and opened the hatch. She jumped out, slipped, and landed on her side. She scrambled to her feet and reached out, toward the lock, waiting for one of the oxygen tanks.

"Give me one," she said. "Let's get going." She turned and began a loping run to the outcropping, leaping twenty feet at a time. She'd land and push off again, sailing across the asteroid. She reached the outcropping in seconds but had trouble stopping. She dropped to her butt and used her free hand to dig at the surface of the asteroid. She managed to slow herself and finally stop.

The others had gathered at the entrance to the outcropping. She dropped the space tank, which floated down, bounced up, and then settled to the surface.

"Nothing here," said Ellis.

Hunter stood staring into the outcropping, suddenly unsure of what to do.

"Let me and Ellis take the oxygen tanks in," said Coollege. "You can wait here, listening to us."

"No," said Hunter. "I don't want to split up."

"You were so all fired in a hurry. Time's wasting now," said Coollege.

"We don't have to go off half-cocked," said Hunter. She stared down, into the outcropping. She raised her voice slightly and called over the radio, "Liz? Call you read me? Do you read me?"

"We've lost contact with them," said Coollege.

"Shut up. I'm trying to listen."

For a moment there was no sound other than Hunter calling to the lost team and the heavy sound of Hunter's breathing. She moved forward, into the outcropping, one gloved hand up on the side of the entrance.

"I can't see anything," she said.

"Let's get going," said Coollege impatiently.

Hunter straightened up and turned around so that she was facing the rest of the team. "I want to stick together. I want us all together in case something happens. We'll have a better chance for survival if there are five of us."

Hunter reached down and picked up one of the spare tanks. She tucked it under her arm as if it weighed nothing. She realized that she was sweating heavily and could feel it dripping down her face and on her sides, making her body itch. She squirmed, trying to scratch but couldn't get anything to rub against her body to kill the itch.

"Come on," said Coollege, starting down into the darkness of the tunnel.

"We stick together," said Hunter. "I'm warning you."

"Okay," said Coollege. "We understand."

She moved through the entrance, saw the opening on the far side and the slide decline. She moved to it, stopped to examine it, and then began the descent.

"We stick close together," said Hunter.

"Right."

On the shuttle Stone heard the last message though it wasn't clear, the rocks shielding the communication. He had climbed back to the flight deck where he had the best view of the outcropping and the team as it walked across the surface of the asteroid.

When they vanished into the interior, Stone used his radio to make contact with the *Lexington*. He didn't say much, only, "The second team has entered. I have lost visual and radio communications with them."

"Roger. Keep us advised."

Stone stood up, and then found himself a bottle of water. He ripped off the cap and sucked on it, drinking deeply. The cold liquid pooled in his belly. He lowered the bottle and wished that he had some alcohol to put in it. He wished that he were with the EVA team because he didn't like sitting behind, by himself, safe, while the others risked their lives.

He rocked back in the pilot's seat, watching the outcropping, knowing that neither of the EVA teams would reappear. The chronometer ticked off the seconds, first noting when the initial team would run out of air, and then when the second.

He realized, as the time slipped away, that if the second team had not found the first, then half of the people outside had to have died. There wasn't enough oxygen to support all nine of them.

"Shuttle One, this is *Lexington*."

"Go, *Lexington*," said Stone.

"Say status."

"Wait one." Stone picked up the other mike and said, "Hunter, can you read me?" He waited, but there was no response at all. "There is no change in status."

"Roger. You are ordered to return to *Lexington*."

For an instant Stone wasn't going to respond. Finally he said, "Negative."

"There is nothing that you can do there. Time has expired. Return to home base."

"Wait one," said Stone. He glanced around the cockpit wildly, searching for a solution that he knew wasn't there. He rubbed a hand through his short-cropped hair and realized that he was sweating heavily.

"You are ordered to return to home base."

"Roger," snapped Stone. He glanced to the right, toward the outcropping where both Price and Coollege had disappeared. He'd worked with them for more than a year and had never left them behind. They were a team, and although one might sacrifice the others, there would be a reason for that sacrifice on the asteroid. He was in no danger and there was no reason for him to abandon his post.

"Advise when ready to launch."

"Roger." Stone decided that he had no intention of leaving. Not unless he was given a good reason for it.

Stone turned and looked into the rear of the shuttle. There were two more suits and half a dozen oxygen bottles. He could take them to the outcropping and leave them.

And then he realized it was a stupid plan. If they could get to the outcropping, they would be able to radio him for help. If they weren't in the outcropping, then no amount of oxygen would help them.

"Shuttle, we are still waiting for your launch sequence initiate."

Stone took a deep breath, stared at the radio control head, and could think of nothing witty to say. His orders were clear and his options were limited. There was nothing he could do on the asteroid alone. They'd need another ship with additional personnel to collect the bodies.

"Beginning the sequence now."

"Roger."

Stone fired up the electrical circuits that had been shut down on landing, checked the fuel on board, and then used the radio a final time. "Hunter, are you in range? Can you hear me now?"

The answer was the quiet hiss of static over the earphones.

Satisfied that he wasn't leaving anyone in the outcropping where he could reach them and rescue them, Stone touched a button that fired the tiny jets directly under the nose, wing hard points, and tail. The shuttle lifted off gently, gliding into space over the asteroid. When he was two hundred meters above it, he pivoted and ignited the main engine.

The trip to the *Lexington* was no shorter than the trip from it and it seemed to last longer. Stone was sure that the fleet was moving away from the asteroid. But the real problem was that he was alone on the shuttle and while he had assistance on the flight over, he had none on the return.

When he approached the shuttle bay, he slowed, waited until the main door opened, and then eased his way through. The deck of the *Lexington* seemed to come up to meet him, but that was only the powerful magnets, turned on by the control room that drew the shuttle down and locked it on the deck.

As he shut down the various systems, he looked out the windows and saw the reception committee coming through the main hatch. Stone leaned back in the seat and took a deep breath. It wasn't going to be easy.

Stone was pacing the conference room, unable to sit down.

The energy that he had forced himself to contain on the flight from the asteroid had bubbled over. He couldn't sit. He kept walking to the portholes and looking out into the blackness of space.

All he could think of was his friends still on the asteroid, maybe needing his help. He forced himself to think in that way. He didn't want to think about them lying dead somewhere inside it. He thought of them needing help, waiting for rescue, while he paced the conference room. The brass hats were sitting on their hands, pretending to have the answers, but it came down to politics. No one was going to make a move that might be wrong now. Not with the loss of the entire crew of the mission. Review boards and investigative committees would be assigning blame and no one wanted it to be pointed at him.

But that did Stone no good. The energy kept him on his feet as he tried to think of something. He felt lost, unable to do anything.

Finally they decided to get the meeting started. They called up the computer-generated holo of the asteroid. Stone watched it for a moment.

The Colonel sat calmly at the head of the table, his leather-covered notebook in front of him. Over the center of the table a holo of the asteroid slowly spun.

"You were there," said an officer. "Yet you can't tell us anything about it."

Stone, still wearing his flight suit with the lieutenant commander rank on it, whirled. He waved at the holo and snapped, "You see it right there in as much detail as can be seen."

The Colonel looked at Stone and said quietly, "Let's remember where we are and what we're doing here. Now, why don't you sit down."

Stone complied and then said, "You have to understand, sir, that I've just lost a couple of very good friends . . ."

"We've all lost friends," said the Colonel. "Sometimes that can't be helped. It will do us no good to violate procedures or to recklessly rush into action."

"Yes, sir."

The Colonel studied the rotating ball and asked, "Is there anything else that you can tell me?"

"No, sir," said Stone. "It was solid, slippery metal, pockmarked, with black stone outcroppings apparently shielded. Radio transmissions did not penetrate them. I heard nothing once the last member of the team disappeared inside."

"Okay," said the Colonel. "There will be a complete debriefing with the scientific staff once they've had the opportunity to review the various sensor tapes and logs. Then they'll want your firsthand impressions."

"When do we go back?" asked Stone. "There is always the possibility they're still alive."

The Colonel closed his leather folder and put the cap on his pen in slow, measured movements. He studied Stone for several moments and then said, "Do you really believe that?"

Stone let his eyes slide away. "No, sir, I don't suppose that I do."

"Then the last thing we need to worry about is speed. Nothing we do will bring them back alive, but if we exercise some care, we might not lose any others."

"Yes, sir," said Stone.

"Gentlemen," said the Colonel, "are there any other questions or comments?"

"Commander Stone," said a naval officer who didn't seem to know that Stone was actually an intelligence sergeant, "are you positive that you did everything you could?"

"Yeah." He looked down at the highly polished surface of the table. "I could think of nothing else which was why I returned. After the air supplies had run out there didn't seem to be anything else to do. I could sit there forever, but they wouldn't show up."

There was a quiet chime at the hatch and it irised open. An ensign entered, centered himself carefully, and said, "I hope that I'm not interrupting, Colonel, but I have a message from the bridge."

"Relay it, please."

"Yes, sir. It seems that the asteroid has changed its course and is swinging away from the fleet."

"What are the Captain's intentions?" asked the Colonel.

"He has received permission from the Admiral to follow, but not too closely. We'll be leaving the fleet."

The Colonel stood and said, "We have a great deal of work to do. Let's get at it."

The others in the conference room came to attention as the Colonel moved to the hatch. It irised open and he disappeared through it.

CHAPTER 6

Once through the first of the metal doors, the rescue team pushed forward with Hunter in the lead. She had grabbed as many lights as she could carry, and then had led the team toward the outcropping. The team stuck together as they walked down the incline, turning with the bends in the tunnel and then continuing on. In the distance they saw a flash of light but didn't know that it was what had drawn Sladen in.

They reached a door, solid metal that was set across the tunnel. Hunter played one of her lights over the door and then the wall but could find no switch or trigger. There seemed to be no way to open the door.

"They must have gotten through here," she said, crouching at the base of the door.

And then, almost as if in response to her words, the door shot upward, into the ceiling.

Hunter used her light, but could see nothing on the other side, except more tunnel leading down, toward the interior of the asteroid.

"What do we do now?" asked Grant.

"The first team has to be down there. We continue on until we find them."

"What about the door?"

Hunter looked up, at the slot in the ceiling, and said, "It seems to respond to our presence. It shouldn't be a problem."

"Yeah," said Coollege.

"You want to wait on the other side?" asked Hunter.

"I'll stick with the team," said Coollege.

Hunter handed her a light and said, "Then please lead the way."

Coollege switched it on and flashed it around the interior of the tunnel. There was nothing extraordinary except for the bright metal of the tunnel floor. It looked as if the tunnel had been carved from solid rock and then the floor had been paved sometime later.

They walked a hundred yards and came to a second metal door. Rather than look for a switch, Hunter centered herself on it, waited, and when nothing happened, she said, "Open Sesame."

The door seemed to respond to the ridiculous command, disappearing upward into the ceiling, as the first door had done. Sladen and Price stumbled forward. Sladen fell to one knee and Price pointed.

"Watch the other door," shouted Price.

Hunter spun and as she did, the far door slammed shut. They heard nothing, and there was only a hint that it had closed because of the darkness inside the tunnel, but they felt the vibration in the soles of their feet.

Coollege turned her light on the door and then took three running strides toward it, but the light was reflecting from the smooth surface of the metal.

"Trapped," said Sladen.

"I didn't know," said Hunter. "You had to be down here."

"That didn't mean you had to foolishly follow," said Sladen. "You could have left someone at the far end."

"Why didn't you?"

"Because," she said, knowing that it was no real answer for the question.

"We brought spare oxygen," said Hunter.

Sladen laughed, the sound more of a snort over the intersuit radios. "That's not going to solve the real problem."

"You bring any tools?" asked Jackson.

"Or weapons?"

"Just the oxygen," said Hunter.

Coollege broke in and asked, "Have you seen anything interesting?"

"We stopped at the door. We didn't want to take it any deeper because we thought there would be a rescue party," said Price.

"And there was," said Hunter.

"Some rescue," said Price. "We're still trapped in here with no way to alert the fleet."

"We brought oxygen," said Hunter again.

"I think we'd better get the tanks switched," said Sladen, "and then we can worry about getting out."

One by one they changed the tanks so that the first team had another two hour's worth of oxygen. With that finished, and with it obvious that they weren't going to get the doors to the surface opened, they decided to move deeper into the asteroid. They had checked the walls, door, ceiling, and floor. They could find no way to open it, and it didn't seem to be responding to their presence.

"We'd better go deeper," said Sladen.

"I think we ought to wait here," said Hunter. "Then we'll be in a position to warn the next rescue party."

"And who is that going to be?" asked Price. "Stone? He's all alone on the shuttle. He'll need to get help from the fleet and before it can get here . . ."

"Then we go deeper," said Sladen.

"I don't see what good that'll do," said Hunter.

"Hell, it can't hurt," said Price.

Hunter took a step toward the door and reached out, touching it with the tips of her fingers. She could tell nothing about it except that the metal seemed to be smooth.

Over the intersuit radio, Hunter said, "We can't just leave here without searching for a way of opening the door."

"We tried long enough. We've been over every inch of it and the surrounding wall," said Price. "You think that if we could have found a way to open it we'd have stayed here."

"We stayed hoping to catch you before you were sucked in like us," said Sladen. "Now we should move deeper into the interior. It's the only thing we can do."

Hunter stood with her back to the group, looking at the solid door. She raised a fist and hit it. That was like striking a vault door. It was obvious they wouldn't be able to smash their way through it with the few tools they had brought with them.

"Maybe we should leave part of the group here," said Hunter.

"No," said Price sharply. "We'd all better stick together now. It's our only hope."

"Whatever we're going to do," said Sladen, "we'd better make a decision because we're running out of time."

"All right," said Hunter. "We'll go lower. Deeper."

"I'll take the point," said Price. Without waiting for a response, he headed down the tunnel. The light on his helmet did little to chase the gloom, the light absorbed by the soft, black rock of the cavern walls. Price was aware of the others around him from the sounds of their breathing coming over the intersuit radio.

The tunnel turned back, to the right, and then, in the distance, was a flickering of multicolored lights. Price stopped and waited as the others came around the corner.

"What's that?" asked Sladen.

"Don't know," said Price. "Let's go take a look."

"Wait," said Hunter.

"Oh, bullshit on wait," said Price. "We're running out of time here and if something doesn't change, we're not . . ."

"I'm aware of the problem," snapped Hunter. "You don't have to keep reminding me."

"Well, somebody do something," said Barnes, his voice an octave higher than normal. "Somebody better do something pretty soon. This arguing . . ."

"Take it easy, Henry," said Sladen. "We'll get something worked out here. Just give us a few minutes."

"We should press on," said Price. "If there is an answer, it's in front of us."

There was a low moan from one of the people and Barnes sat down in the middle of the tunnel. "There is no answer," he said. "No answer."

Hunter said, "Captain Price, why don't you press ahead with the others. I'll stay here with Dr. Barnes. We'll be along in a few minutes."

"We'd better all stay together," said Price.

"Go ahead. See what is in front of us," said Hunter.

"Liz?" said Price.

"Let's go."

Price started toward the dim, flashing lights. He stopped and turned, seeing that the majority of the team was behind him. Before he could speak, Coollege said, "Hey, it's something to do."

Price understood that. They could sit down, like Barnes, and wait to die, or they could push on and see what happened. Price knew that the odds were heavily stacked against them. What could there be in the middle of an asteroid that would provide them with oxygen? That was what they were going to need. Food and water were nonissues simply because they would be dead of suffocation long before they could starve to death or die of thirst.

But rather than sitting down to die, they could continue to explore. It might use the air faster, but what difference would ten or fifteen minutes more make one way or the other. Stone couldn't get to them and the fleet was too far away to provide assistance. In front of them there might be something . . . there might be a way out.

As they walked down the tunnel, the lights became brighter until they separated into a triangle of spots rotating slowly.

There seemed to be nothing significant about them, other than they were lights and were rotating.

Price had focused his attention on them and wasn't aware that he'd stepped out onto a balcony until he walked into the waist-high railing. He grabbed out, afraid that he was about to fall, and grunted in surprise.

"What?

"Everyone stop."

As he spoke, lights all around them came on. A ring of them set into the stone forty feet above his head. He had walked out onto a balcony on the second floor. Over him were another four levels and below was a deck of solid metal that gleamed in a dim blue light. The walls of the first floor were ringed with computers, or what appeared to be computers. On the floor in front of the machines were reclining chairs and next to them were long, rectangular objects that looked exactly like coffee tables.

Sladen stepped to the rail, looked down, and said, "What in the hell?"

"Don't know," said Price.

The whole area was enormous, circular, and at least one hundred yards in diameter. Though there was no sign of a crew, or any other life, everything looked bright and clean and freshly serviced.

"Well?" said Sladen.

"Let's go down," said Price.

To the right they found a spiral staircase that was made of crystal. It looked delicate but seemed to be indestructible. The risers had a strange slant to them and seemed to have been made for something other than the human foot.

When they reached the deck, Price walked to one of the computers, reached out as if to touch it, but then didn't. He watched the flashing lights on the front, wondering if there was some discernible pattern to them. He turned and looked upward, toward the ceiling where there was a bright circle of lights. Then, on the second level, he spotted the rest of the team.

"What have you found?" asked Hunter.

"I haven't the faintest idea," said Price.

The rest of the team straggled down to the main floor. Ellis, the computer expert, walked up to the machines and stood in front of them, staring at them. He just stood there, his hands at his sides, saying nothing.

Coollege sat down on one of the chairs but didn't say anything. Grant and Sladen were walking around the perimeter of the area. Jackson and De Anna were standing together, talking quietly about what they had seen. Their lowered voices came over the radio and sounded like a low-grade hiss to those not paying any attention to them.

Barnes was alone in the middle of the floor. His breathing was rapid and ragged. The faceplate of his suit was misted with his respiration. He was on the verge of panic but had said nothing since Hunter had dragged him down the tunnel and out onto the balcony.

"We've got about fifteen minutes left," said Coollege, her concern breaking through for the first time.

Hunter moved to a position closer to Ellis. "Steve, don't these machines need air to function?"

"Not at all. They can operate in a vacuum or in a combination of gases other than oxygen-nitrogen." Strangely, he sounded like a college professor lecturing students.

Barnes, his voice shrill, shouted, "We've got to do something."

Hunter asked, "You mean that I can't take my helmet off and breathe?"

"Not based solely on the fact that we've got some working computers in here."

"We've got to do something," yelled Barnes again, almost demanding attention.

"Take it easy," said Price.

Grant asked, "If we light a match, wouldn't that prove there is breathable air?"

"It might," said Price, "if we had a match and could get it out to light it."

Barnes dropped to the floor, his hands at his sides. "You've got to get us out of here," he demanded. "Get us the hell out of here."

"Shut up, Barnes," said Price. "Let us think."

Hunter, her voice now shaky, said, "I understand that intelligent life would only develop on planets with a carbon-oxygen cycle that matches ours. They would have to breathe oxygen."

"That means nothing," said Sladen. "It's theory."

But Barnes seized on it. "You see, there is air in here. There has to be."

"Let's stop and think for a minute," said Sladen.

"There has to be air." Barnes reached for the catches on his helmet. "We're going to die anyway." His voice was quieter, deeper, filled with resignation. "There isn't any time left anyway."

"Wait!" shouted Sladen. "Wait."

But Barnes didn't wait. He twisted his helmet, pulled, and jerked it free from his suit. He held it over his head and took a deep breath. His face turned red and his eyes began to roll up into his head. His chest heaved and it looked as if he was going to pass out.

He then pitched forward, putting out his hands in a half-hearted attempt to break his fall. He rolled to his back, his face a bright red.

Sladen leapt forward, snatched up the helmet Barnes had dropped. As she began to put it back on Barnes, he lifted his hands and weakly pushed her away. "I can breathe," he said.

Sladen rocked back on her heels, holding the discarded helmet in her hands.

As the team stood watching, Barnes grinned weakly. His color improved slightly. "See?" he said. And then fell back.

Hunter pushed Sladen aside and crouched over Barnes. His pulse pounded in his throat, the veins throbbing visibly. He wasn't turning blue, blood wasn't erupting through his skin. There was air and air pressure.

"Jesus," said Ellis.

"That was an incredibly stupid thing to do," said Hunter angrily.

"No," said Barnes. "No."

"I guess we can follow suit," said Ellis.

CHAPTER 7

"We've run into another problem," said the Colonel as he opened up the meeting.

Stone, still in his lieutenant commander disguise, sat at the far end of the table, listening. He'd already volunteered to lead a rescue party and had been told to forget it. The air supplies had run out long ago and no one held out any hope that either of the teams had survived.

Now there were scientists in the conference room including an astronomer and a computer expert. They had been working together, trying to break down the code that was being broadcast by the asteroid.

"I think we've solved part of it," said Dr. Jane Kristianson. She was a round woman with long dark hair who nervously drummed her fingers against the tabletop without realizing it.

"We had recorded and broadcast the message at the asteroid, but that did nothing. We reversed it so that it would be obvious that it wasn't a reflection, and that did nothing. We tried everything we could think of to break it down, and that failed as well."

"Is there a point to this?" asked the Colonel.

"Oh, most certainly," said Dr. Richard Smith. He seemed to be a male version of Kristianson, but he didn't have the nervous habit. He sat with his hands folded in front of him like a polite little boy waiting for permission to go out to play.

"We tried many complicated formulas in an attempt to read the message. It certainly makes no sense to create a message that is so complex that it can't be deciphered."

"But then we realized," said Kristianson, "that it was so simple that we overlooked it. They were broadcasting their numbering system. One. Two. And so on. But they used a base six, which surprised us. We'd figured on a base two simply because a race that could launch a complex space vehicle must be familiar with base two."

"Once we understood that," said Smith, "we broadcast a couple of simple mathematical formulas at them . . . pi, for one, and the original message stopped. It has been replaced with a new one."

"And you've deciphered it," said the Colonel.

"Well, no. We've been working on it for a number of days but haven't figured it out."

Smith waved a hand, almost as if to get everyone's attention focused on him, and said, "It seems to me that this is an intelligence test. They are trying to determine how bright we are and if it is worth their while to attempt to communicate with us. They put out a challenging message and they see if we can figure it out and how fast."

"Makes no sense," said Kristianson, now speaking directly to Smith. "You don't send out a message that would take years to reach a receiver and then have no plan to respond once you have an answer."

"That message only took minutes to reach us," said Smith. "Your point is not worth discussing. Colonel, I suggest that we put all our computer . . . cryptographic analysis on this. It is imperative that we decode that message quickly and respond to it."

"Colonel," said Kristianson, "we must be careful here. We

don't want to give away anything until we learn if these . . . beings are friendly or not."

"That ship is a gold mine to us," said Smith. "Contact with an unknown alien race. The fact that it is out here radiating information makes it imperative that we try to ascertain as much as we can."

Stone shook his head, tired of the bickering between the two scientists. "Colonel, the asteroid is moving away from us. We need to mount our rescue operation."

Smith took up the cry. "Of course, a team of properly trained scientists must be sent out to evaluate the artifact. There is so much that we could learn."

"Dr. Kristianson," said the Colonel, "are you suggesting that this thing might be hostile."

She shrugged and laughed. "That might be a bit melodramatic, but we don't have much information. We do know that eight of your people are missing. Let's not overlook that."

"Oh, for God's sake, Jane," snapped Smith, "you can't draw a conclusion based on such limited information. They may have killed themselves accidentally."

"Better to be cautious," said Kristianson.

"Science does not advance in the face of timidity, it stalls."

"Colonel," said Stone.

"You're right, Commander," said the Colonel. He waited for the two scientists to fall silent and said, "I'd like to thank you for your input here . . ."

"You're dismissing us?" asked Smith, his voice surprised.

"For the moment. As questions come up, you will be consulted, quite naturally."

"What about our work?"

"Please continue with progress reports to my aide. If you find facilities or equipment lacking, please let us know, but for now, we have more pressing problems," said the Colonel.

"More pressing than . . ."

"Dr. Smith, please. I thank you for your time. Now, if you'll excuse us."

Kristianson stood, but Smith remained seated, unable to believe that he was to be dismissed. A lieutenant who had been standing near the door came forward and reached down to touch Smith's shoulder.

"Doctor, if you'll follow me."

Smith turned his attention to the Colonel, but finally stood up mumbling. "I've never been treated like this. The General will hear about it. I'll tell the Captain." Then, with as much dignity as he could muster, he stepped to the hatch, waited for it to iris open, and disappeared.

When he was gone, the Colonel said, "He sounded just like a little kid. He's going to tell. Now, Commander, what has your bowels in an uproar?"

"Sir, I think we need to make another expedition to the asteroid. We've got to put some people on there and find out what happened to Captain Price and Lieutenant Coollege."

"I understand your concern, but I don't want to lose more people. Let's see what the scientists learn before we make any more attempts to land on that thing."

"Yes, sir. I take it that I'll be going along on the trip, when it's scheduled?"

"Are you volunteering?"

"Yes, sir. I am."

"Well, that wasn't necessary because being the intelligent military leader that I am, I had already decided to send the one man who had been on the asteroid back to it. Nothing like firsthand experience."

"Why do I feel like I was mousetrapped on that?" asked Stone.

"I don't know. Anything else?"

"How soon?"

The Colonel shut the leather folder in front of him, signaling that the meeting was coming to a close. "As soon as I decide it is time. I'm going to have all my ducks in a row before I commit any more lives to this. Understood?"

"Yes, sir."

• • •

Price stopped at the base of the crystal staircase and waited for Grant to join him. They had divided into teams to explore the interior of the asteroid and while Price would have preferred to work with Coollege, he said nothing as Hunter handed out the assignments.

Price, with Grant right behind him, climbed to the second level and then walked over to the railing so that he could look down. The rest of the team was standing near the chairs, watching him.

The air in the asteroid, now that they were exposed to it, seemed warm and moist, not the best environment for computers. As Price moved away from the railing and walked along the perimeter of the balcony, the sweat began to bead on his forehead. It rolled down his sides and soaked his T-shirt. His lungs began to ache and he gulped at the air. Although the humidity made it seem tropical, the oxygen content made it seem they were at high altitude on Earth. The slightest exercise soon drained their energy.

Finally, from behind him, he heard Grant gasp, "We've got to rest . . . slow down."

Price stopped, turned, his back to the smooth metal of the wall, and slipped to the floor. His breath was rasping in his throat. He rubbed his hand over his face, wiping away the sweat. Finally he asked, "You ready?"

Grant didn't say anything. Her hair was as wet as it would have been had she just come from the shower. The strands hung straight down, around her narrow face. Her face was red from the strain.

Price pushed himself to his feet and then waited until Grant stood. They walked around the perimeter. There were half a dozen tunnels that looked just like the one they had been in. Price could think of no reason to explore them at the moment. Maybe later, after they understood more about the asteroid, but not right then.

When they finished the circuit, they climbed to the next level and made another circuit but again found nothing of interest. Just like the lower level there were entrances to long dark tunnels that seemed to be duplicates of the one they had used to get caught.

"Maybe the doors at the end of these will open to let us out," said Grant.

"You enter on one level and exit on another?" said Price. "Why not?"

"Why not, indeed," said Price. "Let's go take a look and see what happens."

They entered the tunnel, using the lights on their suits. They walked up a slight incline, which Price found encouraging. They slipped back, to the right, and lost sight of the glow from the central area.

"This is taking forever," said Grant.

"Can't be helped," said Price.

They reached the door. Their lights reflected in the brushed aluminum of the surface. He had hoped the door would open and he would then have an answer, but as he walked up, it remained closed.

Now that they had more time, that they weren't concerned with running out of air, Price slowly examined the door and the surrounding environment. There was no indication on how the door could be opened. There were no electronic eyes, beams, triggers, or switches that he could find. He pulled off his gloves and ran his bare fingers over the various surfaces, but found nothing useful. There was no way for him to open the door.

He decided that he wanted to protect his suit. A tiny rip in it would prevent him from returning to the shuttle, if they could open the doors to get out. He sat down on the smooth floor of the tunnel, well away from either wall, and tried to squirm from his spacesuit.

"Help me get this off."

Together they got Price out of his suit. Grant held it while Price crawled over the tunnel floor searching for a pressure plate that might open the door. He found nothing. Finally he sat back and said, "If there is a way of opening it, I can't find it."

"What about the radio?" asked Grant.

"Shielded in here."

"How about I lean back against the door and see if I can't turn the whole thing into an antenna. That might boost it enough to get through."

"I think the problem is power and not the antenna," said Price.

Grant spoke quietly, trying to raise the shuttle. She listened and repeated the message. Finally she said, "I'm not getting anything."

"I'm not surprised. Of course, we might not be able to receive, but that doesn't mean Stone didn't."

"What good does that do?" asked Grant.

"For one thing, it'll tell him that we're still alive after we supposedly ran out of air."

"So now what?"

"We rest here and then walk back to the center."

"Seems like a waste of time."

Price sat with his back to the door, staring down the dark tunnel. He turned to look at Grant. "We've learned some things that might be important later, and you might have reached Stone on the shuttle."

Finally they got up. Price didn't feel a need to put on his suit but took it from Grant. He carried it back toward the center area. They walked out onto the balcony and looked down at the rest of the team.

Sladen stood up and called, "Anything?"

Price shook his head. "No. Nothing. Another tunnel like the one we were in and another door."

"Come on down so we can figure out what to do."

Price and Grant walked down the crystal staircase and then out onto the main floor. Price dropped his suit and rubbed a hand over his sweat-soaked hair. "It would be nice to have a drink of water right now."

"And something to eat," said Coollege.

"Right," said Price.

"As long as we're wishing," said Sladen, "why not a way out of here?"

"Sure," agreed Price, "right after something to eat and drink."

"How long can we live without water?" asked Ellis.

Price rubbed his chin. "The air in here is humid enough, we might be able to figure a way of sucking some of the moisture out of the air."

"Enough to sustain us?" asked Hunter.

"Who knows."

"Well, we solved the problem of the air," said Hunter. "I'm sure we'll think of something."

Price sat on the floor, his back against the chair. "You know, they got us in here and gave us air, I think that we'll find water."

"Who gave us air?"

"The builders of this thing."

There was a sudden silence and then Barnes asked, "You mean this thing is inhabited?"

"I think there is a very good possibility," said Price.

"You seen anything?" asked Sladen.

"No. It's just a gut feeling."

"Wait a minute," said Ellis, "let's not forget the age of this thing."

"That would tend to rule out anyone or anything being alive on the inside," said Hunter.

Price nodded and then said, "But it is still functioning, and it was responding to our communications."

"Automatic systems could account for that," said Ellis. "They activated when we hit it with radio signals. That would be no problem."

Price remembered the blue mist and knew that it could have been launched by an automatic system. Everything that had happened could be the result of computers and automated systems. But he wouldn't retreat completely. "I just think we should be careful," he said. "Just in case."

Hunter stood up, walked nervously around her chair, and then sat down again. "Shit."

CHAPTER

8

Price woke up slowly, unaware of his surroundings, confused by the heat, but an instant later he was wide awake. Sladen turned toward him and said, "Glad that you could join us this morning."

"You have any coffee?" he asked.

"Nope. No orange juice either."

Price rubbed a hand through his hair, which was damp with sweat. He glanced over and spotted Ellis sitting at the computer, staring up at it.

"He learning anything?"

"No. He just keeps studying it, sometimes he stands up, touches one of them, and then sits down again. Once he tried to look behind one of the machines but then didn't."

"It must be nice to have a hobby."

Hunter walked over and joined them. She lowered her voice and said, "I think that we, meaning the military officers here, have to take charge. We've got to think of something, of some way, to get us out of here."

"Granted," said Price, wishing that Hunter would shut up for a moment. He didn't want to start thinking from the instant

that he woke up. He liked time to wake up fully before he
had to communicate with people. Just a short period before
he had to be friendly and social.

"We'll get her in a few minutes. Right now we're the
senior people and if we're going to survive this, we have
to make a few decisions and organize a few things."

Price sat up, his feet on the floor. Everyone had climbed
out of his or her suit and all were wearing the lightweight
coveralls. All were sweat-stained and looked tired. Price
knew exactly how they felt.

"Do you really expect rescue?" he asked.

"You want a real answer or reassurance?"

Price stared into Sladen's brown eyes. "After a question
like that I don't expect anything but a real answer."

"Okay. I just wanted to know if we could rely on you."

"Don't worry about me," said Price.

Sladen nodded. "Okay. I think there will be a rescue
attempt." She held up a hand to stop the protest. "No, they
won't be coming to get us, but they will try to retrieve the
bodies. Besides, they're going to want to know what makes
this thing tick, so we can expect another expedition and
since we disappeared, the next group is going to be fully
prepared."

"I'll buy that," said Price. "But we have to be ready for
them to blast or burn their way in and that could destroy the
integrity of our environment."

"We can't live in the suits," said Hunter. "Too many ways
of damaging them and we're going to need them to get back
to the shuttle, when it arrives."

"So what do we do until that time?" asked Price.

"I think," answered Sladen, "if we can keep everyone
busy, we won't have much of a problem. At least at first.
Hell, we're all professionals here in one way or another . . ."

"Barnes," said Price.

"Could be our biggest problem," agreed Sladen, "but I
think he'll hold together until we reach another crisis point."

"We've got a major problem with food and water. That

crisis might be two days away," said Price.

"Right," said Sladen, running a hand through her hair. "I think what we need to do is explore this thing carefully as quickly as we can."

"Exploration?" said Price.

"We have got to find out something about this asteroid," said Sladen. "If we can't find a source of water, we're going to be dead inside of a week."

"Have you worked out a schedule?"

"Nothing official," said Sladen. "Sara and I talked about it a little. All we really need to do is keep track of which tunnels we've checked and which we haven't."

"Pairings?"

"Nothing official," said Sladen.

"I'd like to work with Coollege," said Price.

"Why?"

Price grinned. He knew he could give her all kinds of excuses and no one would believe them. Everyone liked to believe the worst about his or her fellows.

"I could tell you that I think it would be valuable to be paired with an astrophysicist, but actually I think she's pretty."

"We don't have time to worry about romance," said Sladen.

Price raised his eyebrows and said, "There is always time for romance."

"If that is the only reason . . ."

"Look," said Price, "there is very little chance we're going to get out of this. The fleet, if they are still near, will take its own sweet time before coming back. Now, I think that Coollege and I could work together well and our training will complement each other. Besides, just make it for one day and then switch the pairings if you want."

"Work with Coollege if you think it'll do you any good," said Sladen.

"Thanks."

● ● ●

Price and Coollege climbed the crystal stairs to the fourth level and stood looking at the doors that ringed it. Not the openings that led into tunnels, but actual doors with knobs. They looked strange there, like something that belonged in a long-forgotten hotel on Earth. Giant knobs of cut glass that took two hands to turn.

Coollege stood back as Price turned the knob and pushed on the door, but it didn't open. He glanced back to say something to Coollege and the door leapt upward, disappearing into the ceiling.

"What the hell?"

"Door opened," said Price. He stood at the entrance looking into the room beyond, thinking of the doors that had tricked them the day before.

"I suppose I could enter and if I can't get the door open from the other side, you can do it from here."

"Come on, Tree, this is stupid. I don't think we should enter any room at the moment. Look inside, check the contents, sure, but from out here."

Price poked his head in. "Looks like a well-maintained lounge. A couple of couches that I can see." He leaned in farther but there was nothing else to see from the doorway.

"Let's survey the whole balcony," said Coollege.

"Let's just get this problem solved," said Price. "I'll step in and after the door closes, try to get out. If I can't do it and you can't do it from outside, go get Sladen and have the whole team rescue me. Once I'm out, you can tell me you told me so."

Coollege stood still and said, "Go ahead then."

Price took a step in and moved away, letting the door slide back into place. He turned and on the wall behind him, set away from the door, was a painting that looked as if it had been done in oils.

"What the hell?" he said, and stepped to it. The colors were all wrong, the ground was a flaming orange, there were red trees, and a muddy sky filled with yellow clouds. In the distance, partially obscured by a pinkish mist, was a city of silvery curves. He stood staring at the painting, reaching out with his right hand to touch it.

The door shot up again and Coollege shouted, "Tree? You okay, Tree?"

Without taking his eyes from the painting, Price said, "Yeah. I'm fine." He turned and looked at the door. "Move back and let it close again, please."

Coollege did as requested and Price stepped up to it, grabbed the knob, and turned. The door disappeared upward again. "Come on in," he said.

As she entered, Price pointed at the painting. "Take a look at that."

"Damn."

"Kind of leaps out at you, doesn't it?"

"You think it is an accurate depiction of their planet?"

"How the hell would I know? I've seen lots of paintings on Earth showing scenes that don't exist on Earth. Maybe their color vision is all screwed up. Who knows?"

"We going to take it with us?" asked Coollege.

Price studied it for a moment and then said, "I don't think so. Not right now. We'll let them know that it's here if someone wants to come up and look at it."

"It's strange," said Coollege. "I feel like I'm looking out a window."

"But it's a painting."

"I know."

Price stared at it, trying to get a better view of the city. He realized that if it was a painting, the fog or mist wouldn't lift no matter how long he looked at it, but still he tried to see through it.

"Maybe we'd better go," said College finally.

"Yeah," said Price.

As they stepped off the crystal staircase, Hunter looked at them and yelled, "Come on. Jo found some food."

"She what?" asked Price as he walked closer. Everyone was sitting around stuffing some kind of brown biscuits into their mouths.

"Food," said Sladen.

Coollege said, "Anyone think that it might not be suitable for human consumption?"

"Grant tried a little taste of one and there was no reaction at all. She took a bite and it didn't make her sick. Cured her thirst. She waited to see if she'd get sick and then ate a little more."

Price laughed as he shook his head. "Didn't any of you ever take survival training. Hell, you have to wait twelve hours or more to make sure an unidentified plant is edible."

"I did what I thought was right," said Grant defensively. "I found it and tested it and brought it back here. There is nothing wrong with it."

Price noticed that the area was filled with the odor of freshly baked bread. Sitting on one of the tables was a stack of crusty brown biscuits. The odor was nearly overpowering, causing Price's mouth to water and thoughts of slow-acting poisons and germ-carrying dough to be forgotten.

Jackson held one up and said, "It's really quite good. A little chewy, but quite good."

"I was tempted to just eat the whole thing," said Grant. "It smelled so good."

Coollege picked one of the biscuits from the stack, sniffed it, and then nibbled at it. She glanced back at Price and said, "It tastes fine."

Sladen was sitting on the floor, her back against one of the chairs, a biscuit in her hand. She held it in front of her face, as if examining it closely before eating. Instead, she said, "That seems to have solved the last problem. We have food, and while we don't have water, these things seem to fulfill that function as well."

"How do you know?" asked Price.

"Because, after I took the first couple of bites," said Grant,

"I wasn't thirsty anymore. I wasn't hungry and I wasn't thirsty."

Price shook his head and watched as the others continued to eat the biscuits. He picked up one, sniffed it, and then took a small bite from it. The texture was like that of old white bread wadded together into a ball. It tasted fine. He couldn't believe that it wouldn't poison them in some fashion, but then, what difference would it make. Without food or water, there would be no way to survive.

"See," said Sladen. "No problems."

"We'll see once this stuff has a chance to work into our systems."

"Pessimist," said Grant.

"Realist," said Price. "I've just begun to wonder is all. First we're about to run out of air and at the last moment we discover air in the asteroid. Now we're about to starve to death and die of thirst, and we are provided with a substitute that seems to save us."

"Meaning?" asked Ellis. He had been sitting away, listening to the talk, and eating.

"It just seems a little too convenient is all," said Price. "It bothers me."

"Look at the computer capability," said Ellis. "Maybe it monitors the needs and provides for them."

"Then why not open the tunnel doors and let us get the hell out of here?"

"I don't pretend to have all the answers," said Ellis. "I'm merely commenting on an observation."

Barnes, who had been ignoring the conversation, said, "We can worry about that later. What's important now is that we have everything we need so that we can hold out until the fleet rescues us."

That stopped the conversation dead. The comment hung in the air like yesterday's dirty laundry. Rescue had not been thought of actively by the whole group because the business of immediate survival had gotten in the way. Now there was

a new consideration. How could they alert the fleet that they
hadn't died when the air in the tanks had run out? Each one
knew that the assumption by the officers would be that they
had died of oxygen starvation.

Price took a big bite of the biscuit and said, "Well, these
are pretty good, but I wish there were some butter."

"Maybe we'll find that later," said Ellis.

And in that moment, they had formed a tacit agreement
that none of them would mention rescue. They'd work to
survive for the moment and rescue could be worried about
later.

CHAPTER
9

They settled into a routine that took up the days. They explored the asteroid, entering each of the rooms, checking them, and then retreating into the center area after several hours. Periodically a team would be sent up one of the tunnels, to the huge metal doors, to see if the situation had changed or if the doors would open. They never did.

In the evenings, or what they designated the evenings because the lights in the center never dimmed and there was no way to mark the passage of days except by periods of sleep, they tried to unlock the secrets of the asteroid, but learned nothing that was useful. Ellis couldn't break into the computers, Jackson didn't understand the geological construction of the asteroid, and Barnes could learn nothing of the chemical composition of the biscuits. They had lots of questions but no real answers.

Even Barnes got caught up in the exploration. But it was Grant and De Anna who caused the change in the situation. They had been working together, heading off in the mornings to explore the tunnels and coming back in the evenings to report. Sometimes it took them an hour or more to get to the tunnels because they stopped in one of the rooms to be alone.

During one of their outings, they found a fully equipped biology lab complete to the tiny cages to hold small animals. It was pristine, looking as if it had never been used, or if it had, then someone had cleaned everything very carefully.

During another they found what appeared to be a tool room though no one understood any of the tools. Some of them looked to be nothing more than clubs, crowbars, and hammers, while others were so delicate it was difficult to imagine what function they would have. They marked the location, planning on returning when the exploration was complete.

Like the others, when they reached the end of the corridors, they came to doors that wouldn't open and were forced to turn back. They checked rooms that were empty, rooms that looked to be filled with maintenance equipment, and rooms that held machines that no one could identify.

One afternoon, after they had been trapped in the asteroid for about a week, Grant and De Anna walked out to the door that had trapped them. Grant had decided that it was important to count the steps back to the central area, hoping that might give her a clue about the size of the asteroid. She believed that they had access to only a small portion of the interior and was beginning to think that there were other areas hidden behind locked doors and corridor walls.

De Anna, on the other hand, didn't care at the moment. He was tired of the brown biscuits, tired of not being able to wash himself, and tired of not having the opportunity for an afternoon pick-me-up in the officer's club on the *Lexington*. He only wanted to get free.

Grant practically dragged him toward the crystal staircase, saying, "Come on, Tom, it'll be fun."

"My idea of fun is not walking down a dark tunnel to a door that I know we can't open."

"We might learn something."

"Which will do us no good."

"Hell, if that's the way you feel, stay here and I'll go myself. It's not like there is anything in the tunnel to attack me."

"If it means that much," said De Anna reluctantly, "I'll tag along."

"Oh, goody," she said sarcastically.

"If you're going to be like that, I won't come."

They climbed the stairs together and stopped at the top looking down, into the central area. Finally, his voice quiet, he said, "I don't like this."

"Why not?"

"I don't know. Just a feeling."

They turned and entered the tunnel. The air inside seemed to be slightly cooler and drier than that in the central area. It was something that Grant had never noticed before. She mentioned it to De Anna.

De Anna, his voice quiet, said, "Maybe that's what I noticed. Something different from normal."

Grant laughed and asked, "Why are you whispering?"

"I don't know. It just seems like the thing to do," he responded.

They walked into the tunnel and began the gentle climb. Grant used her flashlight on the tunnel walls, searching them carefully. She came to an area that looked different from the rest. The rock was smoother and looked as if it had been polished once.

"I think I've found something," said Grant.

De Anna, who was a couple of paces in front of her, stopped and turned. "What?"

"I don't know." She moved closer to the wall, crouched in front of the rock, and then leapt back as the wall seemed to iris open like the hatches on the ship.

"I'll check out the interior," she said.

Looking through the opening, De Anna said, "It's dark in there."

"Maybe it'll brighten once I'm inside. I'll be out in a couple of minutes."

"Hurry it up," said De Anna.

Grant flashed him a smile and ducked through the door. After she entered, the door closed behind her and the lights came on. She was in a chamber that looked like a side room off a cavern and not an artificial cabin, though there were signs of construction on the walls, maybe to increase the size of the area. To one side, shoved back against the wall, was a tiny machine that hummed at her periodically.

Grant stepped to it and crouched in front of it, examining it. She found it warm to the touch, warmer than it should have been. There were no wires leading to it and when Grant tried to pick it up, it sparked, snapped, and shocked her slightly. She jumped back, falling to her rear.

She got to her feet and then reached out to push the machine. Though it looked small, she couldn't budge it with her foot. She sat down and pushed against it, but the machine was heavier than it looked.

There seemed to be no purpose for the machine since it wasn't tied into any wiring and didn't have an apparent antenna. There was nothing she could tell about the machine, except that it had flashing lights on the front of it.

She took another look around the room and then moved to the hatch that irised open for her. She stepped out and said, "Some kind of little machine in there." Looking up, she noticed that De Anna was gone.

"Hey! Tom! Where the hell are you?"

She heard nothing in response except the echo of her own voice. She yelled, "Tom! Where are you?"

She listened to the echoes of her voice die away. De Anna didn't answer her. She thought he might be playing a trick because he hadn't wanted to make the trip. Using her light, she examined the tunnel, but couldn't see where he might be hiding, if he was hiding.

"Come on, Tom. Where are you?"

For a moment she thought she would just head on back, leaving De Anna to his game in the tunnel. But then she decided that he wouldn't do that. Kids might do it, but professionals, trapped the way they were, wouldn't be playing tricks on one another. De Anna must have seen something and gone to investigate.

Impatiently, she waited for him to return, calling to him periodically but receiving no answer. Finally she decided to look for him and started for the far end where the tunnel was blocked by the door that had trapped them.

She moved slowly, looking for signs that De Anna had been there before her. She reached out and touched the tunnel wall once. The black rock crumbled easily under her fingers, leaving a smear of black on her hand and a tiny pile of rubble on the tunnel floor. There were no other traces of the soft black rock on the tunnel floor.

She reached a turn in the tunnel, looked down it, and saw nothing except the gloom. There was nothing down there to suggest that De Anna, or anyone else, had ever walked along it.

"Tom! Are you down there?"

When she got no answer, she turned and started back the way she had come. When she found him, she'd tell him off for leaving her. They had been teamed so that one could watch the other. Her partner shouldn't have left her there. What if she hadn't been able to get the door open again. She'd have been trapped by herself.

She reached the hidden door and sat down to wait for De Anna. She was sure that he would come back, eventually. But she didn't like the waiting. She glanced down the tunnel in both directions, impatiently waiting for De Anna's return. She stood up, leaned against the soft black rock, and then paced back and forth in front of the door, causing it to iris open once or twice.

"Tom! Get your butt back here."

She could imagine him hiding, laughing at the sound of her voice. Then she thought of him sitting around the central area, stuffing biscuits in his face, laughing about her waiting for him in the tunnel.

"Okay. That's it! I'm leaving."

She headed back, still checking the tunnel for signs that he might be around, hiding from her. She hadn't walked far when she spotted a puddle on the tunnel floor. She crouched near it and when she reached out to touch it, her fingers came back wet and red.

"Blood?" she said out loud. She sniffed at it but couldn't detect the telltale copper odor. She wiped her fingers on her clothes and then shouted, "Tom! You okay?"

When there was no answer, she decided that she'd better alert the others. She stood up and took a quick look around. The rock on one side of the corridor seemed to have been raked by something heavy and sharp. There was no blood under it.

She turned, took a single step, and then began to trot down the tunnel. In the dim light she could see that there was nothing in front of her but open tunnel. She rounded one corner, slid to a stop, but that tunnel was as empty as the last. She ran down it, hoping that De Anna was in front of her, playing some kind of sick trick on her, but fearing that something had happened to him. She wanted to find her answer as quickly as possible.

She reached the balcony overlooking the central area. Lying on the floor near the entrance of the tunnel was a scrap of cloth. She picked it up. There was a small red stain on one side of it.

She walked to the railing and looked down into the central area. On the far side Hunter and Ellis were still in front of the computers. She hurried down the stairs and over to Hunter.

"You seen De Anna lately?"

"He's supposed to be with you."

"We got separated."

"Now how in the hell did you get separated?" asked Hunter. "You're supposed to stay together."

Grant held out the piece of bloodied cloth. "I found this at the tunnel entrance."

"What's that?"

"I don't know. Looks like blood on this end here."

Hunter took it and examined it. "Yeah, I think that's blood." She looked at Grant. "You didn't see anything?"

"Nothing. I was in a small room, a chamber off the main tunnel. When I came out, De Anna was gone."

"We'd better begin a search immediately," said Ellis. "If that is blood, there is enough there to suggest that Tom has been badly hurt."

Hunter rubbed her face with both hands. She realized how tired she was. It was the strain of being trapped on the asteroid with no idea of when rescue would come. It was the strain of being helpless. It was having to depend on the asteroid for food and water and all the other essentials of life.

"As soon as the others return, we'll organize the search. Maybe someone has already found him."

Grant stepped back and sat down on one of the chairs. "Tom is hurt."

"We don't know that," said Hunter. "Besides, we can't begin an effective search until the others are here."

At that moment Price and Coollege appeared and hurried down the crystal staircase. Price stopped near Hunter and asked, "Where are the others?"

"Out exploring. Why?"

Price held out another piece of bloody clothing. Grant grabbed it and said, "Where'd you find it?"

Price hitchhiked a thumb over his shoulder. "In one of the corridors off the second balcony. Looked as if something had been dragged for about fifty or sixty feet and then the tracks stopped."

Grant was on her feet. "That's got to be where Tom is. It took him there."

"What in the hell is going on?" asked Coollege.

"De Anna is missing and Grant found a twin to that cloth you've got," said Hunter.

"We'd better go check," said Price.

"Weapons," said Coollege.

"What do you suggest?" asked Hunter.

Price said, "At the moment we don't need any weapons. De Anna probably hurt himself and was delirious. All we have to do is follow the trail and we'll get to him."

"In time?" asked Grant.

"Hell," said Price, "I don't know. Depends on how badly he's hurt and how hard he is to find."

Grant hesitated and then said, "I thought I saw something once. In the distance. Something moving but I didn't say anything about it."

"What?" asked Price.

"I don't know. A shape. A dark shape, but I couldn't be sure. It might have been a shadow."

"Why the hell didn't you say anything?" asked Coollege.

"Because I wasn't sure. If it was nothing, it would do no good to mention it. If it was something, then it would show itself again and someone would report it."

"Okay," said Hunter, now angry, "if anyone sees anything, it will be reported to the whole group. We keep nothing to ourselves."

"Okay," said Grant. "Sorry."

Coollege, who was sitting on the floor and thinking about the disappearance, was also staring at the computers. She believed that the answers to their questions were hidden in the computers so she asked, "We making any progress here?"

Ellis shook his head. "I need to find a way to access the machines. A way to input and to ask questions. So no, I'm not making any progress."

Grant interrupted angrily. "We've got to go find Tom. That's our only priority now."

"Right," said Hunter.

"Why don't Grant, Coollege, and I return to the upper level and begin to look around. As the others return, you can send them up if we haven't come back yet," Price suggested.

"I don't like this," said Hunter.

"Neither do I," said Price, "but I think we'd better do something about De Anna as quickly as possible."

"There's something going on here," said Hunter. "We haven't uncovered all the secrets yet."

"No," said Price, "we haven't uncovered all the secrets, but we will."

Hunter nodded and then said, "Good luck."

"I hope that we're not going to need it."

CHAPTER
10

Stone sat outside the admiral's conference room, a handheld computer in front of him so that he could read the latest electronic novel. He could have been reading intelligence updates, news of the fleet, or watching an old-fashioned movie, but he had opted to read a novel. That occupied more of his mind but he was getting more than a little worried. He'd watched a long progression of naval officers enter the conference room, but there hadn't been a single Army man called in, not even the Colonel.

There was a buzz at the yeoman's desk and he looked up. "Commander, you may go in now." He turned his attention back to his work.

"Any Army people going to be here?"

"No, sir. Just the Admiral and some of his staff. And you, of course."

"Of course."

Stone let the hatch iris open and stepped through. Had this been a formal meeting, he would have reported to the officer in charge, giving his name, rank, and telling them he was reporting as ordered. But then, that was the Army and he wasn't sure that the Navy followed the same procedures. And he wondered if officers did it the same as the enlisted troops. It was a question that had never crossed his mind.

The men and women in the room, six of them, were arranged on one side of the table with the Admiral sitting in the middle of it. In front of him was a computer screen but Stone couldn't see what was on it.

The Admiral was an old, balding man with a fringe of white near his ears. His uniform was perfect. He glanced right and left and then said, "We have no record of a Lieutenant Commander Stone with this fleet."

Stone didn't say a word. He stood there, in front of the table, and waited. He wished he could sit down but didn't want to violate protocol.

One of the two women said, "Why is it that you are the only one to return from the asteroid? You were the ranking officer on the shuttle?"

Again Stone didn't speak.

The Admiral snapped his fingers for attention and then asked, "Did you understand the question?"

"Yes, Admiral."

"Then answer it."

"Technically I was the ranking officer on the shuttle, but Sladen had overall command of the mission. When she exited with the first EVA team, command devolved to Hunter. It was her decision to take the remainder of the people out when the first team failed to return."

"What do you mean technically?" asked one of the other officers.

"It means quite naturally that there is a good reason why you have no record of a Lieutenant Commander Stone. I am currently assigned to an Army unit."

The other woman spoke. It was obvious that she was outraged. "Then by what authority do you wear a naval officer's uniform here?"

"Admiral," said Stone evenly, "I think this could all be cleared up if you would contact my colonel."

"At the moment, Mr. Stone, we're only interested in having some of our questions answered, especially since a number of naval officers are dead, not to mention several civilians assigned to us."

Stone took a deep breath but didn't speak. He'd been told, in the first of the intelligence training sessions he had ever taken to never volunteer information to those who didn't have it. He didn't know what the Admiral had been told or how much coordination had been made by the Colonel with the Admiral. Until he heard something from the Colonel, he decided to keep his mouth shut and volunteer nothing more.

"You heard the question, Mr. Stone?"

"Yes, Admiral, I heard it."

"And the answer?"

"Am I to be represented by legal counsel?"

"Do you need it?"

Stone, feeling slightly sick to his stomach, the sweat beading on his forehead and beginning to drip. He wanted to wipe it away, but knew that any sign of nervousness would prove to those watching him that he was weakening. He stared into the eyes of the Admiral.

"Could you call the Colonel?"

"There is no need, at this moment," said the Admiral, "to involve anyone in the Army for any reason that I can see unless you care to enlighten me."

"No, Admiral."

"Isn't it curious," said the first woman, "that you are the only survivor of the mission?"

Stone had the perfect answer for that, given the circumstances on the asteroid, but he said nothing. He stood at attention, staring at the Admiral.

"Are you going to answer?"

"Is there a point to it?" asked Stone.

"Just who in the hell are you?" snapped another of the officers.

Stone thought that he could ask the same question. He recognized none of the officers facing him except the Admiral and he didn't know the Admiral personally. He was now caught in the vacuum between one command and another. He was not authorized to tell anyone who he really was.

"Commander," said the Admiral, "if you refuse to answer any of our questions, I am going to put you into the brig until such time as you decide to cooperate. You will remain there indefinitely."

"Admiral . . ."

"Nine people are dead. You were the senior officer on the shuttle. We are trying to determine what happened to those nine people."

"I appreciate that, Admiral, but I am not responsible for their disappearances. I was not the overall mission commander, nor did I have a choice about returning to the *Lexington*. I was ordered off the asteroid."

"You were only following your orders and were not in overall command so you don't feel responsible for the deaths of those people."

Stone was quiet for a moment. "No, sir, I do not. I did my job as well as I could. The decisions that led to the problems were not my decisions."

"The captain of a ship is responsible for everything that goes on around him even if he didn't create the problem himself."

"Yes, sir, but I wasn't the captain of a ship. I was a shuttle pilot."

"The pilot is like the captain of a ship."

"While in flight, yes, sir. But we were landed and Sladen as mission commander had taken over."

The woman took over and said, "Then you are blaming Sladen for the disaster."

"Admiral," said Stone, "I'm not trying to place the blame on anyone at the moment. I'm merely pointing out the reality of the situation."

"Commander Stone," said the Admiral formally, "I am not satisfied with your answers. I believe that some time in the brig might make you more cooperative."

Stone grinned quickly. He knew that the Colonel, the moment he learned about the situation, would get him out. He was doing his duty and if the Colonel needed to speak to the General and have him speak to the Admiral, it would be done. He'd get out, return to his duties as a sergeant, and no one would ever mention the Lieutenant Commander who had been the shuttle pilot on the mission where so many people had died. He'd disappear just as the rest of the team had done.

"Admiral," Stone heard himself saying, "if there is another mission to the asteroid, I'd like to go."

"Why is that?"

"Well, the disaster wasn't my fault. No procedures were violated, no rules broken. I was ordered to leave and had I stayed, there was nothing that I could do. But if there is a return mission, I want to go. I want to find out what happened there."

"You will remain in the brig until you decide to answer our questions," said the Admiral.

Stone shrugged and said, "Yes, Admiral."

The brig wasn't overly uncomfortable. The bunk was bolted to the bulkhead and had no mattress in the steel frame. There were no bars on the door, but an electronic field that stunned anyone who came into contact with it. Stone might be able to leap through it, but it would be an hour or more before he would be able to move again. Even if he didn't set off an alarm by leaping through, surely someone would check within that hour. There would be no escape.

He sat on the bunk, elbows on his knees, and carefully watched the deck. He was taking it easy, relaxing, knowing that someone would come. If he had learned one thing in the Army, it was patience.

The Colonel appeared in front of the electronic screen and shook his head. "Why is it that I am always having to get you out of trouble?"

Without looking, Stone said, "Because fieldwork requires a few chances here and there. We operate on the spur of the moment so things sometimes go wrong."

"Sergeant, I have an order for your release. I can get you off this ship now."

Now Stone turned and looked up at the Colonel. "But?"

"I have had a chat with the Admiral. He knows the whole story now. He knows exactly who you are." The Colonel grinned broadly. "He was more than slightly annoyed."

"I can imagine."

"However," said the Colonel, "the Admiral is willing to forget and you can retain your naval rank for a little longer. He has been convinced that there was good reason for all these behind-the-scenes maneuvers."

"But there is a catch."

The Colonel turned and waved a hand at an unseen guard. The electronic field vanished with a staticlike popping. The Colonel hesitated, letting the residual radiation dissipate, and then stepped through into the cell, glanced at the bunk but continued to stand. "You'll be on the next shuttle mission to the asteroid. If there is a next mission."

"Which is what I wanted all along."

The Colonel grinned. "Their feeling is that you should be required to return. Sort of like the mechanic who is required to test fly the aircraft before it is returned to active service. Make sure that it is working properly."

"I demand the opportunity to return to the asteroid," said Stone.

"Rocky," said the Colonel, "this isn't going to be as simple as it sounds. We've already lost people and we don't know why we've lost them."

"But we go with weapons and tools."

"And more people. Two or three shuttles with everything needed to ensure the survival of the people going in. Everything carefully planned to the last detail. We don't want to lose anyone else."

"I want to go," said Stone.

"Then you need to go back into that room and tell the Admiral what he wants to know. He needs to save face."

"I kept my mouth shut because I wasn't authorized to tell him anything."

"Now you are. You will not tell, and he won't ask, about your real identity. If the question comes up, you ignore it and let the Admiral deal with it."

"Yes, sir."

The Colonel said, "They'll be by in a few minutes to get you and take you back."

"Yes, sir."

"Anything you want to know?"

"Have we learned anything new about that damned asteroid yet?"

The Colonel shook his head. "It is broadcasting a message that we have yet to figure out. The scientists figured out the first, which was little more than a numbering system."

"Yes, sir, I know that."

"But it is continuing to broadcast the second message. The scientists haven't been able to figure out the second. They're content with that . . . receiving the messages."

Stone took a deep breath and turned his attention to the deck again. It seemed ridiculous for them to be attempting to return to the asteroid without having more information. It seemed ridiculous to risk more lives when there was no immediate pressure to do so.

"The asteroid is picking up speed," said the Colonel, almost as if he had read Stone's thoughts. "It is moving away from the main line of the fleet and there is no doubt that the *Lexington* will be recalled. All the information will be logged and if anyone gets back out here, they'll look for the asteroid."

"Colonel, we have the first evidence of a spacefaring race we've ever found."

"And our scientists are doing everything they can now, but we have other missions."

"I would think there would be a great deal more excitement about this."

The Colonel stepped to the bunk and sat down. "The scientists are excited about it, but they believe there is nothing to be learned from landing. The information is being broadcast to us. They'll be able to keep it under observation and they can work on deciphering the codes of the messages. They're happy as clams."

"We are going back?"

"Soon," promised the Colonel. "I believe that we will be mounting another mission soon."

"Good."

CHAPTER

11

They tried to find De Anna, but had no luck. They searched the area where Price and Coollege had found the bloody rag, but there were no other signs of him. With Grant, they walked back to where she had last seen De Anna. They examined the tunnel floor where she had found the blood, the tunnel near the hatch she had found, and then had walked on to the door that blocked the entire tunnel. Price counted the steps as they returned.

It took them a couple of hours but they found nothing to suggest why De Anna had vanished. He was completely gone and though there was nothing to suggest the blood was his, there was no other place for it to have come from.

As they walked out onto the balcony, Coollege asked, "What do you think happened to him?"

"I don't know. Maybe he saw something and wandered off to check it out. Remember, he is a scientist, not a soldier. He wouldn't be thinking the same way we do."

"Then you're not worried?"

"At the moment I'm not worried. Concerned, yes, but not worried."

"What about the blood?"

"There could be a dozen ways to explain that. Maybe he got a nose bleed and couldn't get it stopped easily. Maybe he cut himself and couldn't get the bleeding stopped."

"That's a hell of a lot of blood."

"That it is."

They walked down the crystal stairs. The others were standing around waiting. Ellis and Hunter had told them that De Anna was missing. Hunter came forward and asked, "You find him?"

"No," said Price. "And I guess your question means that you didn't either."

"No. And none of the others did either. No sign of him anywhere."

Price said, "I did notice one thing, it's farther to the doors than it is to any other of the barriers we've encountered."

"Who cares?" snapped Barnes.

"Well," said Price, "for one thing, it tells us that there are areas that we haven't been able to penetrate. De Anna might have stumbled into one of them and gotten trapped on the other side or is confused."

"Then we'll never find him," said Barnes. "We can't get to the other side."

"Well, there is always the possibility that we can find our way over there too," said Coollege.

"Except that we don't know where it is. It's been hours. He could have been bumbling around anywhere. That's if these other areas even exist," said Grant.

"Don't be stupid," said Price. "You know from the outside dimensions of this thing that we haven't seen a fraction of the interior. I'm merely suggesting that we've been sealed out of a great deal of it."

"You suggesting that there might be another intelligence on board?" asked Barnes.

"No," said Price, "though that is not an unreasonable assumption given those computers."

But Barnes wouldn't let go that easily. He said, "That's

what you think. You believe there is something in here with us, don't you?"

Price glanced at the others and then said, "I don't think that. There is no reason to believe that. If Ellis is right about the age of this thing, then I see no way for anything to be in here but us."

"Your logic doesn't work," said Barnes.

"Logic has very little to do with it. It is observation that answers the question. We have seen nothing to suggest that we are not alone."

"Except that Tom is missing," said Barnes.

"But Tom could be missing because he screwed up. We don't need to invent some kind of an extraterrestrial menace to explain his disappearance."

"This is doing us no good," said Sladen.

Hunter said, "I have some thoughts on this." Then for several seconds Hunter didn't say anything. She sat with her eyes closed, tugging at the fraying cuffs of her flight suit. Finally she said, "There are two real choices here. One, there are other compartments in other parts of the ship set up for the collection of specimens. This ship, roaming between the stars, somehow draws the specimens to it . . ."

"There are some interesting possibilities there," said Price, interrupting.

"That doesn't make sense," said Jackson.

"No, think about it carefully," said Hunter, her voice suddenly hard. "For it to travel among the stars with no return is wasteful . . . or for it to travel with a single success is wasteful."

"Unless the galaxy has little in the way of intelligent life. Our success in finding them has been limited," said Jackson.

"True," said Hunter, "but for the moment, that doesn't matter because of the second possibility. There is a sealed crew compartment in here. They'll remain sealed until they determine if we're dangerous or not."

Jackson laughed out loud. Hunter turned to Coollege, still

believing that she was an astrophysicist. "What do you think about it?"

"Other specimen areas. Don't want to contaminate one sample with another," said Coollege.

"Anything in them?"

"Who knows? Could be loaded, could be empty, could just contain the remains."

Hunter looked at Price. "You think that De Anna fell into one of those other areas?"

Price thought about it and then said, "No. The blood suggests an accident."

"Yeah," said Coollege. "As I said, they'd be sealed to prevent contamination."

"Then we'll have to break through," said Hunter.

"I'm not convinced that would be a good idea," said Jackson. "At the moment we're in the same boat as the creators of this thing. We don't know if the . . . creatures . . . in one of those other areas would be friendly. Hell, they might carry bacteria that would kill us."

Barnes said, "The probability of alien bacteria being dangerous to us is very remote."

"What the hell does that mean?"

Barnes found himself in the center of attention for the first time. He stood up and moved around as if he were a college professor lecturing a group of freshmen. Of course, his field was chemistry and not biology.

"There are some bacteria that can be transmitted from animals to humans. AIDS might be one. There is a theory that it developed in lower primates before spreading to humans. Rabies is another example. But there are diseases that will kill snakes that have no effect on humans. The biological systems, though evolved on the same planet, are that different."

Barnes grinned and said, "And when was the last time that a human contracted wheat rust or corn blight? The point is that I don't think we need to worry about that. It's probably the least of our worries."

"There is one thing that we all seem to be forgetting," said

Price. "If Ellis is right, this thing is fifteen thousand years old. If there was anything living on it, it has died long ago. We've seen no signs that anything survived."

"That doesn't mean they haven't," said Ellis.

"Let's not borrow trouble," said Price. "Without some observational data suggesting there is life on this, why assume it now."

"This is all very interesting but it doesn't find De Anna," said Grant.

"I think we're going to have to let him find us," said Hunter. "There are just too many areas where he could be and we just can't search them all. He can't have gotten out of here and by trial and error he'll get back, probably hungry and thirsty and madder than hell."

"Why mad?"

"Because we didn't find him."

Price realized that they had finished their discussion of De Anna. He said, "Not wanting to change the subject, but has Steve had any luck with the computers?"

Ellis spoke for the first time. "I'm afraid that we have been overly optimistic about that. I've seen a lot of computers, I've done a lot of experimental work on them, but none of it seems too useful here."

"You know," said Price, "there is one thing that has been bothering me. We kind of touched on it, but we haven't thought about the real question. We've found a bunch of small cages for animals. That would suggest originally there was someone around to go outside and collect those samples. The question is, who was supposed to collect those samples?"

Hunter said, "That is a very interesting question. A very good question."

Price said, "There is something else going on here. Something we don't understand."

"Meaning what?" asked Hunter.

"I don't know."

Hunter looked at the group around her and decided that they had exhausted the topics. "I don't think there is much more for us to do right now. Let's get some sleep and then tomorrow we can try to open one of the locked doors."

Coollege stood up and said, "I don't like this. It's too much like those intelligence tests we used to take."

No one paid any attention to her.

Ellis found himself alone in the center room, the computers continuing to flash. He had done everything he could to the outsides, had studied them carefully, and could find no way to do anything to them. If he was ever going to learn anything, he was going to have to try to open one of them. When the others, climbing into their spacesuits, had taken everything out of their pockets, Ellis had kept a small group of tools in his. Like any professional, he kept the tools with him. The small leather case didn't take much room and presented no danger to him.

Ellis carefully removed the front panel of one of the computers and found a shelf in it, looking as if it had been designed to be pulled out and swung to the right. Ellis laid his tools on the shelf, arranging them carefully, and then stepped back to study the interior. There was a pulsating light near the top that seemed to have a rhythm that was different from the rest of the machine.

But that was almost the only thing that he recognized. He had hoped that the interior would have printed circuit boards but it didn't. There were clear panels hanging inside that seemed to have no connection from one to the other. Grooves had been traced on them, looking like maps of rivers with all their tributaries, but nothing that could double for wiring, bubble memories, or transistors.

There were tiny holes on the boards and Ellis stuck a screwdriver in one of them and twisted. There was momentary resistance and then it yielded. He pulled and the panel opened until he saw a variety of small things hanging behind it that looked as if they were tools. He picked one up, examined it, and then stuck it into one of the holes. It turned easily.

"Now we're getting somewhere," he said.

He worked his way down the front of a panel, across the bottom, and then up the other side. He reached in, pulled. The panel shifted. He finished along the top, holding on, but the panel didn't come out when he pulled.

Stepping back, he noticed another small hole in the side. The tool he held would not fit in, but one of the small, corkscrew-shaped ones did. As he twisted it a full turn, the panel fell free, dropping to the bottom of the computer and then falling out.

He took it out and saw that the light at the top of the machine continued to flash. He then pulled the next panel free and finally the one behind it, but the light still flashed.

"Okay," he said. He took out all the plastic panels, stacking them up on the deck. As he pulled the last one free, the light went out. He'd finally been able to interrupt the circuit. He wasn't sure what good that did, but he felt a sense of accomplishment. Now, if he could put it back together and get that light to flash, he would have learned something about the internal construction of the machine.

He lifted the last of the panels he'd removed, slipped it back in, used the corkscrew, and fastened it to the top. He had expected the light to begin to flash as he pushed the panel in, but that didn't happen.

He removed it again, examined it, and wondered if he hadn't inadvertently inverted it. He set it aside and leaned into the computer and let his fingers play over the interior of it. Finally he stepped back in disgust. He had believed that he was going to find some kind of radio, transmitter, booster, or the components of a computer, but there wasn't one thing that he recognized. He reached up and touched strands of what looked to be gold and silver suspended in midair. He had no clue as to their purpose.

Ellis had about given up for the moment. He had been unable to reassemble the machine so that the light would begin flashing again. He tried to replace them in the correct order, just as he'd taken them out, but failed. The light in the corner would not begin to flash again.

While he was sitting there, the others straggled in looking exhausted. They silently spread out and flopped into any of the chairs.

Hunter took a deep breath and asked, "How'd it go?"

"Not very good." He waved at the machine. "I got it apart but can't seem to get it back together."

"Like the little kid who took apart mom's watch," said Price.

"Exactly," said Ellis. "How'd you all make out?"

"We couldn't budge it. We barely scratched it. I don't see how we're going to break through with anything short of an atom bomb," said Sladen.

"De Anna?"

"No sign of him," said Hunter. She leaned back and pinched the bridge of her nose.

"Maybe all this is just a waste of time," said Barnes. "They're probably working on rescuing us right now."

It was the second time that he'd brought up the topic. This time Price could not resist the challenge. He looked at Barnes and said, "They think we're dead. If we're to get out, we're going to have to engineer it ourselves and then let them know we're still alive."

"How?" asked Jackson.

"I would think," said Hunter, "just getting to the surface would do it. They'll be studying this thing and any change we can make on the surface will force them to investigate."

"But we don't need to worry about that yet," said Price. "First we have to find a way to penetrate the door."

With that, they all fell silent. They were too tired to talk at the moment, too tired to think.

Deep in the bowels of the asteroid, under the tiny center section that could have been called the cockpit, had there been a crew to use it, and hidden behind what appeared to be more computer modules, was a miniature room. Near the middle of it was a plastic and chrome box that was only slightly larger than a coffin, and inside it was an almost human-sized creature. A creature with two arms that ended in long slender fingers that could be called tentacles. Both the legs and the arms were covered with a thick fur, but only to the knees and elbows. Fur also covered the feline face from the throat to the back of the neck. Two large, yellow eyes were closed in a sleep that had lasted for more than nine thousand years.

When the computer and keyboard in the fourth sample confinement area failed, it tripped an alarm on the central computer bank. That computer tried, unsuccessfully, to correct the problem and when it couldn't, it initiated the arousal cycle for the maintenance man, if such a title was applicable to a being from another world.

The supercold gases that had induced the state of suspended animation were rapidly sucked from the box and replaced with warm, sterile air. The fluids that had been pumped into the creature when it entered the box were now drained, replaced with its equivalent of blood. Another machine began a pulsation that simulated a heartbeat, for the being had a circulatory system that was remarkably humanlike.

As the creature warmed, electrical impulses were transmitted through the body at various points, at first simulating normal body activity, and then stimulating it. Slowly the creature became aware of its surroundings. It felt cold, then cool, and finally warm. But that was really all it felt at first. Then consciousness seeped back in and it realized that it was in a confined space, that it was lying down, and that it had been asleep for a very long time.

When the creature was fully awake, the lid lifted automatically and one side fell away. The being swung its legs out, and stood up stretching. The tendons, ligaments, and muscles popped and creaked, but the long period of slumber had not noticeably reduced the muscle tone. The creature glided forward, opened the door, and moved into the cockpit to find out what had happened.

CHAPTER
12

Ellis had become convinced that the secret to escaping from the asteroid was hiding in the computers. With the help of Jo Grant, he began to peel the front panels off all the equipment that ringed the central room. Grant helped when she could, holding panels, handing Ellis tools, and offering suggestions that Ellis frequently ignored.

While Ellis worked with Grant, the others continued to explore the interior of the ship. They knew that there was empty space inside it, if they could penetrate the interior walls to get into it. And they continued the search for De Anna, though most believed that he must be dead. If he wasn't, he wouldn't have remained missing. He would have found some way of letting them know that he had survived.

Although the others found nothing new, Ellis believed he was making some progress. Nearly every one of the machines had some kind of light inside that suggested the machine was functioning properly. He learned how to remove the clear plastic boards using one of the tools that he hadn't understood at first. It looked like a brass rod, tapered at one end and blunt on the other. The engraved circles around the big end apparently generated some kind of an electrical field that interrupted the magnetism that held the boards in place. Whenever he removed one with the brass rod, the light went out. When he replaced them, using the rod, the light went on again.

Ellis wondered if there might be a way of discovering some kind of transmitter and using it to contact the fleet. But all that ended when they pulled the front from one of the machines and found what they could only believe was a huge keyboard containing several hundred push buttons. By loosening the screws with the brass rod, he could swing it down so that it sat in front of him like the keyboard of a computer on any of the ships.

He examined it closely, running his fingers over it like a pianist who had just been given a baby grand. He touched the keys lightly, rubbing his hand along the sides and bottom of it, trying to find any bumps, dents, or protrusions. When he finished, he sat back and stared at it, trying to spot something that he might have missed during his first examination of it. The only thing he hadn't done was push one of the buttons.

Grant was getting impatient. "Do something."

"What?"

"I don't know. Push one of the buttons. Maybe that will start something."

"I've already thought of that. I'm thinking about it."

"What's to think about."

Ellis knew that she was right. There was nothing to lose by pushing a button or a series of buttons. He let his fingers dance lightly over the huge keyboard. Finally he pushed one and a tiny light came on marking it. He pressed it again and the light went out.

"Now what?"

"I'm waiting to see if it does anything," said Ellis.

But the computer did nothing. It sat there waiting for Ellis to do something. Ellis knew the keyboard was tapped into the computer and if he could figure out a way to communicate with it, he might be able to learn to program it.

"Try a square," said Grant.

"Why?"

"Well, you can't talk to it in English, but a square would seem to be a universal. If you have spaceflight, you have to know about squares. You have to understand some engineering and you have to understand geometry."

Ellis shrugged. "Why not?"

He pressed the buttons in the center of the keyboard creating a square. He sat back and said, "It's up to the machine now."

For a moment nothing happened. Then the lights blinked once and went out. All of them, across the entire keyboard, flashed in a strange, incomprehensible pattern, as if the computer were cycling itself and digesting the information. Eventually it stopped, leaving only a few lights in the middle, shaped like a right triangle, glowing.

Ellis studied them briefly and grinned broadly. "Obvious." He pressed the buttons on the top and sides rapidly. "Pythagoras."

From that point they worked through a number of geometric patterns and mathematical theorems. Always the computer would erase one and replace it with another, always with something that needed to be added. Ellis filled in the blanks. It was as if the computer were testing Ellis, trying to find out how much math he knew. Or to discover how intelligent he was.

Finally the computer created half a geometric shape and stopped. Ellis waited but nothing was added. He finished it, thinking they had taken a step backward, but still nothing happened. The lights burned steadily, not changing, not blinking, neither adding nor subtracting from the figure that Ellis had created.

"What happened?" asked Grant.

"I think we broke it."

The rest of the team straggled in an hour later. Sladen dropped into the closest of the chairs and rubbed her swollen feet. She noticed that Ellis had taken the panels off all the computers and saw the keyboard pulled out near one of them. She took a deep breath and asked, "What's happening here?"

Ellis pointed. "That is a keyboard."

There was a moment of silence and then Price suddenly shouted, "Then we're out of here!"

Cheering erupted from the others. Ellis stood holding his hands up and tried to outshout them. "Wait a minute. Wait a minute." When the others fell silent, he said, "There are some things about this that you should know."

"Such as?" asked Coollege.

"It'll only work up to a point and then stops. I think there is a flaw in the programming and I haven't been able to work around it."

"Will you be able to?" asked Barnes.

"Yeah. Probably."

"How soon?"

Ellis sat quietly and rubbed a hand through his hair. "There are so many things that I don't understand about this. Right now I'm playing games with it, not programming. There's a lot that I'll have to learn before I can get into that." He sat for a moment and then said, "I have had one thought. We've had incredible luck."

"What does that mean?" asked Hunter.

"Haven't you been thinking. Doesn't it seem a little strange that everything we've needed for our survival has been handed to us. First we need oxygen and minutes before ours runs out, we discover breathable air in here. Not exactly perfect, but certainly adequate. Then we need food and water and we discovered one of the rooms holds a machine that manufactures a biscuit. Not visually pleasing, but tasty enough to eat. Not only does that solve our food problem, but also our water problem because they have enough water in them for our survival. Then we find a room filled with tools. Nothing we're familiar with, but a room of tools nonetheless. And then we find the computer keyboard hidden inside a machine . . ." Ellis looked at his companions, but they seemed to be unimpressed by his analysis.

Sladen broke in impatiently and snapped, "So what's the point here?"

"Point? I'm not sure that I have a real point. It has just struck me as strange that we've been handed everything we need since we got trapped in here. We've been very lucky."

Price listened carefully, remembering his thoughts of the last few days. "Hold it," he said. "I think the point is that this whole thing, this asteroid, has been set up to take care of the problems as they come up. But more importantly, it sucks us in, and holds us here like some kind of giant rat trap."

"Oh, Jesus H. Christ. That is the most ridiculous thing that I have ever heard," said Jackson.

"Think about it," said Price.

"I have thought about it," said Jackson. "Your analogy breaks down. The purpose of a rat trap is to kill the rats. That could have been done in the first two hours. Hell it could have done it in the first thirty seconds."

"There are humane traps," said Price. "The rats get themselves in and then can't get out. Food and water is supplied and they are then moved to an environment where they aren't a nuisance."

Sladen laughed out loud. "It's more like a rat maze. All we have to do is figure out how we can escape from it. Our reward is our freedom."

Price snapped his fingers. "That's it. This whole thing is an intelligence test."

"Then we're being watched," said Barnes.

Jackson shook his head. "Not necessarily. Besides, we've seen no evidence of that."

"But we're all being analyzed in some fashion," said Coollege.

Sladen slumped back and realized that they were right. She thought of the variety of rooms they'd found from a biology lab to something that only could be viewed as a fully equipped pathology lab.

"Let's accept that for a moment," said Ellis. "Let's say this is a giant intelligence test. The question becomes, how do they get the results? The answer is by radio. They know the path it's taking and they just monitor that portion of the sky, waiting for some kind of results."

Price suddenly felt sick to his stomach. Suddenly they were supplying an unknown race with information about humanity. He said, "So, in other words, this thing is radioing data about us to some distant star."

Ellis said, "I wouldn't worry about it. If they had the capability to get here, they wouldn't have sent only a robot probe."

"Don't be too sure they haven't," said Hunter.

Ignoring that, Ellis said, "You have to admire their ingenuity. It only discovers intelligences that have spaceflight."

"If they went to all that trouble, then they must be monitoring us," said Grant.

"I would imagine so," said Sladen. "They would want to know everything about us."

A blush started at Grant's neck and crawled up her face to her hairline. She glanced sideways at the others but said nothing about what she and De Anna had been doing in some of the out of the way rooms.

Sladen interpreted the blush correctly. "I guess they know more about us than I thought."

Ellis said, "This is all speculation. We don't have any facts to back us up."

"No," said Price. "But it all makes sense. It provides them with a quick way to explore the galaxy without having to invest in a great deal of wealth in the exploration. If something is discovered, then they can figure out whether or not they want to follow up on it."

Barnes had been sitting quietly but suddenly jumped in. "You people are sitting here talking about it like it is some kind of test designed to learn our responses and that we'll get out of here soon . . . when the test is finished."

"Take it easy, Henry," said Sladen. "At the moment there isn't much we can do."

"We can talk about getting out," shouted Barnes. "We can try to get out."

"And do what?" asked Sladen.

"Let the fleet get us out of here," said Barnes. "Let them know that we're alive."

"Relax," said Price. "Right now we've other things that must be done."

"Such as?" snapped Barnes.

"De Anna's still missing," said Price. "We don't know what happened to him."

"De Anna's gone," said Barnes. "We've got to worry about ourselves."

"Shut up!" yelled Grant. "You don't know a damned thing. Always whining about yourself." She stood and faced the others. "None of you has taken any of this seriously. You haven't done anything to find Tom . . ."

Sladen stepped to the younger woman. "Sit down, Jo."

Price asked, "What would you have us do that we haven't done? Just because there have been no results doesn't mean we haven't been trying."

Now Barnes said, "We should be trying to get out, not sitting around discussing this."

Sladen nodded. "Unfortunately, I think that Henry is right on this one."

"I've been working on that," said Ellis. "But, at the moment, the key seems to be broken."

"You don't think this thing was built by the lowest bidder, do you?" asked Price.

Sladen said, "That would certainly explain some of the problems we've encountered."

"A higher intelligence would see the flaws in such a system," said Price. "Maybe they would have it built by the contractor with the best record."

"But it is fifteen thousand years old," said Sladen.

"Which might account for some of the problems that we have encountered."

"This is incredible," said Barnes, his voice high and tight. "First we're trapped in here. Then you people sit around making bad jokes. And now when we seem to figure out a way to escape, the damn thing breaks."

"Yeah," said Ellis. "Ironic, isn't it?"

CHAPTER

13

Sladen decided that they had to find De Anna. That was the priority because they were in danger until they found out what happened to him. If they didn't know, it could happen to another of them. She decided they would split into teams and they would carefully search for De Anna. That was the only mission they would have. Once they learned the answer to that question, they could concentrate on finding a way to get out.

Sladen suggested that one military officer accompany each group so she changed the structure. She left Price and Coollege together not realizing that Coollege was a military officer. She also decided that she would go with Barnes, figuring he would be the hardest to control. Grant could stick with Ellis, which left Hunter and Jackson working together.

Once she had these assignments made she said, "The plan is to go back to the two places where the bloodied clothes were found and radiate out from there. We structure the search so that we cover everything. We do nothing that will get anyone else hurt. Any questions?"

"If we find something?" asked Jackson.

"Mark it and return to this point immediately. We'll explore anything like that together. I don't want anyone else disappearing on us."

"Maybe we should all remember to be very careful. We don't know what happened to him," said Price.

"But no one has seen anything," said Barnes. "There's nothing to worry about." He sounded as if he was trying to convince himself.

"Anything else?" asked Sladen, ignoring Barnes.

"Guess not," said Price.

They walked to the crystal staircase and Sladen turned. "Good luck, Steve."

Ellis was already sitting at the computer keyboard, studying it carefully. He raised a hand and waved without looking. "Thanks."

At the entrance to the tunnel, where Grant had found the first scrap of bloody cloth, they stopped. Sladen looked down the tunnel and said, "We can assume that he is not back by the main door. Grant had to come from that direction to find the cloth. Now, what I think we should do is split up here, some of us going one direction and some in the other. I think we should meet back here in a couple of hours. If you find anything, return here immediately."

"That's going to slow down the search," said Price.

"I don't want to take many more chances."

"Okay," said Price. "I'll take Hunter and Jackson with me."

"And come back here immediately if you find anything," she said again.

As the four moved off, Barnes said, "That leaves just you and me."

"We'll be okay. Come on."

They walked around the perimeter of the balcony until they found a long passage that led deeper into the asteroid. They stopped in front of doors that opened when they centered themselves on it. They checked the interiors, made sure that

De Anna hadn't somehow trapped himself in one of them. Satisfied, they moved on.

They checked a dozen rooms, some of them vacant and some of them filled with equipment they didn't understand. But they were searching for De Anna and not alien machines. They ignored everything as they made sure that De Anna was not hidden in some corner and when they found that there was no evidence of De Anna in them, they moved on.

They found nothing unusual. They finally reached as far into the corridor as they thought they should go. They decided that it was time to return to the main balcony.

When they came to the first main corridor, Price said, "Why don't you and Jackson take this one. I'll go on with Coollege."

"Fine," said Hunter.

Grant and Jackson started off, walking carefully, slowly. They moved from one section to another and as they did, the dull, blue lights came on.

They found more rooms with doors that irised open just like those on their own ship. Most of the new rooms were empty, but they did find a couple of small machines that seemed to be working, but neither could determine what they did.

They came to a branch in the corridor and Jackson asked, "What do we do now?"

Grant peered down one and then the other. She pointed at the left branch and said, "I think this goes deeper into the center of the asteroid."

"So?"

"You take one branch and I'll take the other."

"We shouldn't split up," said Jackson.

"What are you afraid of? There's no one around here but you and me."

"That didn't do De Anna any good. He's gone although there was no one else around."

Grant felt her anger flair at Jackson's argument. She wanted to strike out at him. "That was not my fault."

"And I never said it was. The point is that we don't know what else is happening in here. We shouldn't split up. That's all I mean."

Grant took a deep breath and said, "If we stay in the lighted areas, in the center of the corridor, and retreat at the first sign of anything suspicious, we should be okay. Besides, if we don't split up, it's going to take forever to complete the exploration."

"We have the time," said Jackson.

"If you were De Anna, injured somewhere, would you be happy with that attitude?"

"It'll do him no good if more of us disappear."

"Let's just do this my way," snapped Grant.

Jackson looked as if he was going to respond and then just shook his head. "I don't like it."

"Be careful and you'll be fine," said Grant.

Jackson stood staring at her for a moment and then turned, walking down the corridor. He glanced back once and then continued on.

Grant watched him for several seconds and then entered the other corridor. She was worried about all the wasted space, thinking of the troubles caused on a ship while they tried to use every square inch efficiently, but then decided, with an asteroid more than a mile in diameter, a little wasted space didn't matter all that much.

She'd walked about a hundred yards along the corridor when she thought she heard something. She stopped and listened, but there was no other sound around her. She started again, heard the sound again, and stopped again.

Her first thought was that Jackson had changed his mind and was trying to catch up to her. She turned, looking back, but there was no one in the corridor with her. Just the empty tunnel that stretched into blackness.

The sound came again but this time it was followed by a high-pitched shriek that set her teeth on edge. There was a third, quieter, subtler noise that sounded almost human. It sent chills down her spine.

There was a scream that had to be Jackson. It was a scream of pain and fear and she knew that she had made a mistake by insisting they split up. She ran down the center of the corridor, slowed as she neared the junction, and then stopped, listening for more.

She heard another scream that was choked off in the middle. She moved to the side, her back against the rough wall, and slipped to one knee. There was no more noise.

She stood, and reached back, a hand against the wall. She started forward slowly, trying to hear anything else and trying to see through the gloom. Her eyes dodged right and left as she searched for anything out of the ordinary. Far away, she thought she could hear the scrambling of claws on the rock flooring of the tunnel.

As she approached the junction, she stopped, leaned back, and closed her eyes, trying to hear anything, no matter how faint. The noise faded and when she peered around the corner she saw a dim shape, a shadow, that seemed to swim in and out of view. There was a hint of two legs, maybe four, and a massive trunk that was two or three times the size of a human. It vanished into the blackness at the far end of the corridor.

She stayed where she was and whispered, "Hey, Frank? What's going on?"

She moved into the center of the corridor but there was no longer anything to see. "Frank?" she called, her voice low, almost inaudible because she didn't know what was in that corridor. "Where are you?"

The skin on the back of her neck crawled, stretched tight and itching as fear crawled in her belly. She felt her ears twitch as she tried to hear everything around her. Once, convinced that she was being stalked, she spun, but the tunnel behind her was empty.

She knew that she was alone. She knew that she should retreat and find the others. She knew that something was wrong. But she forced herself forward, searching for some sign of Jackson.

Ten yards in front of her she found a small pool of blood. It was a black puddle on the corridor floor. She crouched and reached out, touching it. She lifted her fingers, holding them in front of her eyes. The odor of hot copper filled the air around her.

Glancing up, she saw more stains on the tunnel floor, and a smear on the wall. She stood and walked forward slowly, following the trail. A few yards later the corridor ended against a wall of solid metal.

When she reached it, she saw that there was some blood on the floor at the base of it, looking as if someone or something had set a bloody body down while the door was being opened. It was more of a smear of blood and not a pool of it.

Grant didn't know how long she stared at the metal of the door. She touched it once, but there was nothing interesting about it. Finally she turned and began to walk her way back to the junction. She avoided the blood, staying close to the opposite wall.

At the main tunnel she found Price and Coollege sitting on the floor, talking quietly. She ran up to them and said, "I've lost Jackson."

"What?"

"Jackson's gone."

"What happened to him?" Coollege asked.

"I don't know," said Grant.

Price held up a hand and said, "Slow down. What in the hell happened?"

"We came to a junction and Jackson took one side and I took the other," said Grant.

"Wait a minute," said Coollege, "I thought we were to stick together."

"We thought we could speed things up a little bit," said Grant.

"And now Jackson is missing . . ."

Price cut in. "Let's just try to find out what happened here."

"He disappeared," said Grant. "I heard him scream and I found some blood. He's gone. Behind a door."

"God damn it!" said Coollege.

"How long ago?" asked Price.

"Ten, fifteen minutes."

Price was on his feet. "Let's get back there."

"There's nothing there now," said Grant. "He's gone. Just some blood."

"What in the hell is going on here?" asked Coollege.

"We've got to get back there," said Price. "Look around." He turned and looked directly into Grant's eyes. She was slowly slipping away from them. Shock was beginning to set in. She'd been with De Anna when he vanished and now Jackson was gone in a similar way.

"Won't do any good," she said. "No good."

"We've got to try. All of us. If we stick together, then we should be safe."

"There was something else," said Grant. "Something moving in the corridor."

"What?" asked Price.

Grant ran a hand through her hair, pulling it away from her face. "I don't know. A shadow in the distance. Maybe humanoid, maybe not."

"Oh, for God's sake," said Price.

"I didn't see much," protested Grant. "Just something far away. It wasn't Jackson . . ."

"We still have to go search for Jackson," said Price. "It's the only thing we can do."

Grant slipped to the corridor floor and shook her head slowly like a great dog that had captured and finally killed a rabbit. It was all in slow motion. "Won't do any good," she said. "No good at all."

"Emma," said Price quietly. "Take her back to the central control room."

"Just what do you think you're going to do?"

"Search for Jackson."

"No!" screamed Grant. "That's what happened before. I sent him off on his own and he vanished completely. It'll happen to you."

"That's ridiculous," said Price.

Coollege said, "I don't think that it's a good idea. What ever is happening, it happens to loners. Why take the chance?"

"We might have an opportunity to save Jackson."

"And you might disappear," said Coollege. "And there's that shadow that Jo saw."

"If she saw anything," said Price.

"We should get back to the main cabin," said Grant, "and tell the others. Tell them about the creature. All of us should go in search of Jackson."

"What creature?" asked Price, exasperated.

"What I saw in the corridor after Jackson disappeared. We have to be careful of it."

"She's right," said Coollege.

Price stood quietly, thinking. Speed seemed to be important, but then so did caution. Two people had disappeared, both of them alone. The three of them might be able to protect one another.

"Then all three of us should go in search of Jackson."

"That would work," said Coollege.

"No!" said Grant. "We must go tell the others first. We have to go after them first. We have got to warn them about what is happening."

"We're wasting time here," said Coollege.

"We go find Jackson," said Price.

"We have no weapons," said Coollege. "Maybe we should think about that before we go charging off."

Price thought about that. He thought about Grant's description of something in the corridor. Finally he nodded and said, "You're right."

CHAPTER

14

"I don't fucking believe it," screamed Sladen. "The orders were perfectly clear. Everyone sticks together until we learn exactly what happened to De Anna."

"We didn't separate by that much," alibied Grant.

"It was enough," said Sladen, her voice shaking. "More than enough."

Price broke in. "This is doing us no good. We should be trying to find Jackson."

Sladen sat down on one of the couches. She took a deep breath and asked, "What about that creature?"

"We don't know if there was anything," said Price.

"Let Grant speak."

"I didn't see much," she said carefully. "It looked to be about our size with a thick chest. I didn't get a good look at it."

Ellis, who had turned away from his computers, said, "I think we'd better rethink some of the problems. There is no longer a reason to believe that we're alone in here."

"And still no reason to believe we're not," said Price.

"Except that De Anna and Jackson have vanished and Jo said that she saw something."

Barnes was sitting on the floor, his head held in his hands. "You never said there would be something in here to kill us."

"Oh, knock it off, Barnes," said Sladen. "That's not going to help us."

"Weapons," said Coollege. "We need to find something to use as a weapon."

"No weapons," said Ellis. "We use our wits to survive but no weapons."

Price looked down at the scientist. "Sometimes," he said, "there is nothing to do but use weapons. We have to protect ourselves."

"We don't know that we're in danger," said Ellis.

"Pools of blood and missing people suggest it clearly," said Sladen.

"There was that room of tools," said Price. "We could make something there."

"What about Jackson?" asked Grant insistently. "He could be hurt."

Sladen looked at her and said, "Jackson is gone, just as De Anna is gone. We've got to think about protecting ourselves and not worry about those we can't help."

"We're jumping all over the place here," said Price. "We've got to sit down and think our way through this. We've got to plan."

"But we don't know what we're facing," said Barnes.

Sladen stood and began to pace. She studied the deck under her feet. No one spoke for several minutes. She stopped and faced the whole group. "Weapons first and then some rest. We start a coordinated search in the morning. I doubt that we're going to find Jackson alive."

"That's not true," said Grant.

"I'm afraid it is," said Sladen. She spoke softly. "We've got to face reality here. Both De Anna and Jackson are gone. If they weren't we'd have found them . . . we'd have found De Anna. That tells us something."

Price said, "I think it's time that we break into one of the other sections."

"That didn't work before."

"We didn't have the same incentive."

In the central control room, the creature sat down. It stroked the fur that covered its lower arm, combing it as a young woman would comb her hair to make it shine. It leaned back, slowly closing the shirtlike garment that it had put on. It reached out with an arm, extending one of its incredibly long fingers, and wrapped it around a smooth cylinder that had a groove near the top.

A display flickered and lighted, but it was focused on the wrong sample confinement area. The creature changed cameras and then saw the group of humans discussing Ellis's find. Of course, it didn't know what they were discussing. It only saw the strange-looking beings who were trapped inside.

Keeping one large, yellow eye on the screen, it turned to the left, punched a series of buttons, and read the material that paraded in front of it. It ran through the sequence quickly, looking for the program that had failed, but came to an abrupt end. Some of the information hadn't been sent, or hadn't been received. There was no way to tell which.

It reviewed all the activities of the aliens in the sample confinement area, watched as they discovered there would be air to breathe and food to eat. It also learned that they designated one small room for the elimination of waste and wondered why they worked so hard for the privacy to collect their waste.

Finally it switched to the computer run made by the aliens, watched as they used the keyboard to initiate a simple program, and kept it running until it abruptly ended. It was another computer that hadn't been fully programmed. The creature turned off the display, turned to a CRT to call up the schematics of the computers and the software used to support it, searching for the problem. It didn't suspect, at that point, that the fault was not the hardware or the programming, but the programmers.

• • •

The door to the tool room opened naturally as Price centered himself on it. He walked in and stopped, studying the variety of tools spread out in front of him.

Sladen followed him, but Grant didn't. She stayed in the corridor with Coollege. Coollege finally stepped through the door leaving Grant by herself outside the room.

Price moved to the wall and reached out to touch the objects hanging there. Most of them looked like so much junk pasted together to give them interesting shapes, but that had no real function other than to confuse. One by one, he peeled them off the wall and set them aside.

Once that was completed, they all sat on the floor, examining each of the tools. Price found one that was about ten inches long and cigar-shaped except for a flat edge on one side. He pressed it against the palm of his hand but it was dull. He put it down and then picked it up again. He pressed the flat edge against the side of a table and to his surprise was able to cut off a corner.

He sat there for a moment and then said, "That's it. I've got what we need."

"Then let's go find Jackson," said Grant from outside the room.

Sladen nodded and said, "That seems to be the thing to do now."

Before he stood, Price said, "Let's not rush into this. We should take a couple of the bigger, heavier tools for weapons and I think I can sharpen a couple so that we'll have knives and short swords."

They armed themselves with the weapons they had made and then walked toward the door where Jackson had disappeared. Price crouched near it, put the cutting tool against the metal, and then stopped.

"There is the possibility that the chamber on the other side will be a vacuum, or filled with a gas poisonous to us. We'd better be prepared to block the hole."

"Just make a tiny one until we have some answers," said Sladen.

Price shrugged and pressed the cutting tool against the smooth, cool metal of the door. When nothing happened, he moved it slightly. He pulled the tool away, saw a thin mark on the metal looking like a deep scratch. It was slightly warm to the touch.

"It's working," he said.

"Just be careful," said Coollege.

Price put the tool back against the metal and pushed it back and forth, trying to make a hole in the door. Suddenly the tool slipped, as if it had sliced through the last of the resistance. Price leapt back but there was no rush of air, in either direction. He put his hand against it and could feel nothing other than a residual warmth on the surface of the metal where the tool had been working.

"Well?"

"Well, nothing."

Price raised the tool again and began to cut a larger hole in the door. He worked the tool around, cutting deeper and deeper until he'd made a hole about six inches in diameter. He pulled the tool aside and then used his elbow to punch out the disk. He then crouched and peered through the hole.

"Well?"

"Can't see a thing," said Price.

"Open it up," said Sladen.

"Wait," said Grant. "Let's think about this for a minute or two."

"Jackson's over there," said Sladen. "He might be hurt or dying. We have to hurry."

"We don't know if he's over there," said Grant. "We don't know what might be over there. And yesterday you were in no hurry."

"We can get through and we have to do that," said Price, ignoring Grant. "All the answers we want might be over there. It's the first break we've had in days."

"I don't like this," said Grant.

Price glanced at Sladen who said nothing. He raised the tool and began to widen the hole so that they could get through.

Stone stood in the viewing room on board the *Lexington* and watched the distant point of light that marked the asteroid. It was accelerating out of the system, moving away from the line of flight of the fleet. He was facing the port, watching it and wondering what progress was being made by the scientists who were designing the next mission to it.

"Commander?" said a voice behind him.

Stone turned and found Jane Kristianson standing close to him. "Yes."

"We've come to a decision . . . all of us on the scientific board."

"Yes?"

"At the moment we believe that the risk of another landing on the asteroid outweighs the knowledge that we could gain from it. No one on board our ship believes that it would be in the best interest of science to risk any more lives on this. At this time, anyway." She didn't look at him while speaking but stared at the deck as if she'd found something incredibly interesting on it.

"Wrong," said Stone. "We have to go back there."

"Data is still being received from it," she said. "There is no reason to approach it again." She moved forward and reached out, touching him on the arm. "There are defense mechanisms on board the asteroid that we do not understand. It destroyed our missiles and it trapped our people. Until we know more, it is our recommendation that we monitor the craft but we make no more attempts to land on it."

Stone turned and walked to the closest table. He dropped into a chair and put his chin in his hand. "I don't understand you people. Out there is something we have never encountered before. Instead of trying to get to it, you sit here, in safety, and watch it."

"That's the point. We don't have to risk any more lives

but we're still gaining knowledge from it. A landing doesn't change that."

"The Colonel will overrule you," said Stone. "He understands more than you."

"The Colonel will go along with our recommendation," she said. She twisted around the chair closest to him and sat down facing him, leaning closer to him. "I'm very sorry about all this."

"Those were my friends who disappeared," said Stone, knowing that he was revealing something that he shouldn't. To others he was just the shuttle pilot and not an intelligence operative. He supposedly had no knowledge of the people who'd flown with him to the asteroid.

But Kristianson didn't pick up on it. She kept her eyes down, now on the surface of the table. "They're all dead. You know that."

Stone didn't want to admit it. He wanted to believe that they had survived, but if that had been true, they would have returned to the shuttle. He had been holding out, hoping that on the return mission he'd learn that they had survived.

Finally, quietly, his voice barely audible, he said, "I know that. I don't want to believe it."

She touched his hand and then took his fingers in hers, squeezing slightly. "I know that it is hard, but you have to face the truth."

Stone thought of the young captain who had taken over the unit when the old boss had been promoted and ordered to return to Earth. A very young man, unsure of himself, but who had taken control quickly, listening to those around him, and then making solid decisions. A young man who could blend in with others, become one of them, and learn everything about them. A captain who was not really the commander of the small unit, but a friend too.

And Coollege who looked almost too young to be a military officer. She didn't look deadly but she was. She had arrived, thinking that officers didn't speak to enlisted men. It was beneath their dignity. But she had learned that the only way for the intelligence unit to operate was as a team. Each member was important to that team.

As a member of that team, it had been his responsibility to see that all members returned safely. He'd failed on that point. He'd left them stranded on an asteroid and now he was being told that there would be no return flight to it. They would stay there.

"I'm very sorry, Commander, but I'm sure that you see the wisdom in the decision." She wanted to say more but could think of nothing that wouldn't sound trite and insincere. All she could do was keep quiet.

Stone felt tears burn his eyes. He glanced up, at the ceiling, and blinked rapidly until he knew that the tears wouldn't fall. "I see no wisdom. Just an avoidance of the obligation to our friends."

"Nothing would be gained by returning," she said.

And that was the trouble. Stone knew that she was right. Nothing would be gained by returning. Price and Coollege couldn't survive on or in an airless asteroid, and even if they could, there was no food or water for them. They would have died long ago from thirst and starvation. All they could do was go pick up the bodies.

"The plan is to keep the asteroid under surveillance, learning all we can. Eventually we'll return."

"That does no good."

"No," agreed Kristianson, "but then, without the loss, we'd probably not know anything about the asteroid. At least we now know something about it."

"That doesn't help," said Stone.

"I suppose it doesn't." She was quiet for a moment and then said, "Would you like to have a drink?"

Stone shook his head but then said, "Just one."

CHAPTER
15

In his central hideaway, the maintenance man, still watching the antics of the humans, was suddenly alerted by a flashing light and a ringing bell. He turned toward a different monitor and discovered that another sample confinement area was now inhabited.

The creature reached out with its long, slender fingers and touched a recessed button, lighting a new screen. The view of a corridor blossomed, but nothing in it moved. The creature shifted the camera angles and then the cameras, but found nothing unusual. Then it caught a flicker of movement, turned the camera, and saw that the humans had gotten into another of the areas. It didn't understand how the captives in one area had penetrated into another, but knew that they had. It was determined to force the humans back to their original area.

The creature pushed itself out of the lounge, opened a door, and activated a switch. A large panel, concealed behind a dummy computer display, opened slowly and the creature stepped into a central core that looked as if it was a duplicate of the one the humans inhabited in another part of the asteroid.

It moved to the crystal stairway, its feet fitting the strange shape of the riser, and started to climb. Halfway up, it changed its mind and retreated to the cockpit. It sat down to think about what was happening inside the asteroid and what it should do about it.

Without waiting for instructions, Price stepped through the hole he'd made, being careful to avoid the sharp edges and hot metal. He inhaled carefully, found the air to be thin but breathable. The lights popped on and he leaned down, calling, "Come on in."

"You see anything?"

"If you mean Jackson's body, the answer is no. I don't see any blood over here either."

Grant and Sladen stepped through. Price gestured and said, "Looks the same, doesn't it?"

"Come on," said Sladen.

Coollege joined them on the other side of the door. She straightened up, looked around, and said, "It's the same as our side."

"How far do we go?" asked Grant.

"The others don't know where we are," said Price. "I suggest that we don't go very far before we return. Just look around and see if we can find any sign of Jackson."

Together they moved deeper into the new area. The lights came on as they entered each section, some of them very dim. There were sections where it was difficult to see anything even with the lights.

They searched the floor, the walls, and the few rooms they passed but found nothing that told them what had happened to Jackson. The blood that had led them to the door disappeared on the other side.

Price turned to say something to Coollege and caught a flicker of movement out of the corner of his eye. It was just a fleeting image seen at an extreme range. He said nothing to the others.

They continued on, moving slowly, searching. When they

reached the first branch in the tunnel, they stopped. Price asked, "Which way?"

"Maybe we'd better head back," said Coollege.

"Good idea," said Grant.

Sladen whipped her head around and pointed. "Any of you see that?"

"What?"

"Over there. Something moved."

"I thought I saw something earlier," said Price. "Just a hint of movement."

"Then that's the way we go," said Sladen. "Down there."

"Wait!" said Grant. "We're not prepared for this."

"Could be Jackson," said Coollege reasonably.

"Let's go," said Price. He began to run down the corridor, toward the intersection.

Sladen caught him, grabbed him, and said, "Wait. We've got to stick together here. We've got to be careful."

But then the lights in the new section of tunnel came on and they saw it. It stood in the center of the corridor, facing them. It was nearly five feet tall and humanoid in appearance. A bullet-shaped head sat on broad shoulders. The legs seemed spindly and incapable of holding it up. Two thick arms tapered to three-fingered claws.

"Jesus," said Price.

"What the hell is it?"

"I think we know what happened to Jackson," said Price, his voice low so that he wouldn't call attention to himself.

The creature stood its ground, staring at them. Suddenly it lifted its head and there was a high-pitched scream from deep in its throat. It was one of the sounds that Grant had heard just before Jackson disappeared.

It took one short step toward them, stopped, and twisted its whole upper body so that it could see to the side. Then it leapt toward them.

As Sladen retreated, Price stood his ground, the short cutting tool in front of him. He took a step or two forward, but then stopped.

The creature ran straight at him, its claws raised and pointed. As it closed with Price, it swung. Price ducked under the blow and swiped at the belly of the thing but missed. The momentum carried him a step closer.

The alien swung again, with the back of its hand. The blow caught Price on the point of the shoulder, lifting him from his feet and smashing him into the tunnel wall. He bounced from it and rolled to the floor, staring upward and too dazed to move. The cutting tool slipped from his nerveless fingers.

Grant stood rooted to the floor watching the sudden violence. All she could see was the big pool of blood that Jackson had left behind.

Sladen had stopped and turned but didn't move. Coollege ran past her, holding a pointed club in both hands. That inspired Sladen who now ran forward as well. She stopped short, turned her side, and lifted both hands, keeping her fingers rigid.

The creature had lost interest in Price. It met the new attack, lifting its clawed fingers. Sladen kicked out, trying to break the legs, but the beast's claws flashed and caught Sladen around the ankle. It lifted upward and she lost her balance, falling on her back. The breath left her in a coughing whoosh. She tried to roll clear but the alien held on to her.

Coollege swung with her club, hitting the beast on the side. It staggered slightly and with its free arm, claws out, swiped at Coollege's stomach. She leapt to the rear, the claws ripping through her flight suit and the flesh of her belly. She fell, struggled to her knees, and then rolled to the side, out of the way of the creature.

Price was on his feet. He kicked out with all his strength. He hit it just below the shoulders, driving it forward, the head snapping back. It fell to one side, roared once, and swung at Sladen but missed her.

Price whipped around, his cutting tool held out, ready to strike. The beast scrambled to its feet but had no desire to fight on. It fled deeper into the asteroid, the long, loping gait eating up the distance.

Sladen was on her knees in front of Coollege, trying to pry her fingers from her belly. "Let me see it," she said.

Price was standing with his back to them, watching the tunnel, wondering if there were more of the creatures or if it would return. Over his shoulder he said, "We've got to get out of here."

Sladen pulled the cloth of the torn flight suit to one side. There were three gouges across Coollege's belly. The wounds weren't deep, just painful.

"Can you walk?"

"Yeah."

Grant appeared then, crouching near Coollege. Coollege looked up at her. "Where the hell were you?"

Price was retreating slowly. "We'd better get the hell out of here."

"We've given it a path into our side of the asteroid," said Sladen.

"No," said Grant. "That is what got Jackson. I heard its scream on our side of the door. It already knows how to get over there."

Sladen held Coollege's arm and pulled gently as Coollege got to her feet. She stood for a moment, wobbling, and then smiled weakly. "I'll be okay."

Price looked at Sladen. "How are you doing?"

"I'm okay. Just had the wind knocked out of me."

"I guess we know what happened to Jackson," said Price. "That thing got him."

"And De Anna too," said Grant.

"Yeah," said Price.

They began their retreat to the door. Sladen helped Coollege walk. Grant led the way and Price covered the retreat. When they reached the door, Coollege crawled through it first and then sat down, her back against the metal.

Price came through last and found Sladen crouched over Coollege who looked up. "I don't feel good."

"You don't look good either," said Price. He looked down

at her belly. The gray of the flight suit was darkly stained by
blood. Her hands were covered with it.

"She's losing a lot of blood here. I don't think we should
move her anymore."

"We can't leave her here," said Price. "Too dangerous."

"We can kill anything trying to come through this hole we
cut," said Sladen.

"Except that it seems that the creature knows how to get
through this door without the use of our hole."

"Coollege can't walk anymore," said Sladen.

Price crouched in front of her. "How you doing, Emma?"

"I don't feel good, Tree. I really don't."

"Can you stand?"

"Yeah. I think so."

"I told you that we shouldn't move her," said Sladen.
"We've got to stop the bleeding."

Price pulled at the flaps of cloth and looked at the wounds.
They didn't appear to be very deep. It was the motion of
walking that was keeping them from scabbing over. He
looked up, into Coollege's eyes. "Let's get going."

Price put his arm around Coollege and then bent, sweeping
her up into his arms. He shifted her body slightly and asked,
"You comfortable?"

"You can't carry her all the way," said Sladen.

"I can try." He glanced back at Grant. "You cover us from
the rear."

"Sure."

They moved slowly along the corridor, the lights coming
on as they moved into the new sections, the ones behind them
going out. Grant had realized that any movement by the alien,
if it tried to follow, would be betrayed by the lights. All she
had to do was watch for the lights to come back on and she
would have plenty of warning.

They stopped frequently to let Price rest and to check the
wounds. The bleeding had slowed significantly but Coollege
still looked pale.

They finally walked out on the balcony overlooking the

central area. Price set Coollege down. She smiled weakly at him and said, "Thanks, Tree."

"No problem . . . Emma." He didn't use her nickname. It would tell those with them too much. After all, they supposedly met for the first time when they began the mission.

Sladen checked the wounds. "I wish we had some first-aid kits. I don't like the looks of this."

"Or some water," said Price, "just to flush them."

"I'll be okay," said Coollege.

"Of course you will," said Price. He wished he believed what he was saying.

When they reached the main floor and had Coollege resting on one of the couches, the others crowded around. Barnes looked as if he were going to be sick. "What happened?"

"We found something," said Sladen.

"What?" said Hunter.

"Is she going to be all right?" asked Ellis.

"Let's get her taken care of," said Price, "and then we can play twenty questions."

Satisfied that Coollege was in no danger and had been taken care of, that the bleeding had stopped, they all moved away from her to let her rest. Sladen, her voice low, said, "There is something in here with us. Something dangerous."

"Oh, my God," said Barnes.

"You mean something alien?" asked Hunter.

"Of course alien," snapped Grant. "What the hell do you think?"

"Hold it," ordered Sladen. "We've got to think carefully, not attack each other."

"Is it intelligent?" asked Ellis.

Sladen turned to look at him as if he had said something incredibly stupid. "How in the hell should I know that. We were lucky to get away from it."

Price interrupted. "I think that it has some intelligence. It managed to penetrate our side of the asteroid. It figured out a way to get to us."

"Then we're not safe," said Barnes, his voice suddenly very calm.

"We're going to have to find it again and kill it," said Price.

Ellis laughed. "We find an unknown form of life that might be intelligent and you want to kill it."

"Doctor," said Price sarcastically, "it has probably killed two of our people, it attacked us with no provocation, and will probably attack again. What choice do we have?"

"Communication," said Ellis. "Intelligence should recognize intelligence."

"I appreciate what you say, Doctor," said Sladen, "but on this one, I have to agree with Price. There is no chance for communication. It doesn't allow it."

"You probably didn't try," said Ellis.

"No, Doctor," said Price, "we didn't try. We were too busy trying not to get killed."

"So you didn't try," pressed Ellis.

"Shit!" said Price. "No, we didn't try and I'm not going to try. I'm going to figure out a way to kill it and then you can see if it was intelligent. Right now we have no other choice."

Sladen closed her eyes, wobbled, and reached out to support herself against one of the couches. Price leapt toward her and noticed a bruise on the side of her head that disappeared into her hairline.

"You okay?"

"I'm fine. Shaky but fine. I have a hell of a headache and you arguing with everything doesn't help."

"Sorry," said Price.

Hunter said, "I might point out that we don't know that it killed any one of us. All we have are suspicions."

"I think we can assume that both De Anna and Jackson are dead and I think we can assume that the creature we saw killed them. The only thing we can do is kill it before it kills any more of us."

"Our first priority," said Ellis, "is to establish contact. If we work carefully . . ."

"Our first priority," shouted Price, "is to kill the fucker before it kills anyone else. Period."

"Lieutenant Sladen," said Ellis.

Sladen just shook her head and said, "The discussion is over. We kill it. As soon as we can. And we establish a watch on the upper level so that it can't get in here with us while we sleep."

"I don't like this," said Ellis.

Price was at the end of his patience. "I'm getting tired of you, scientist. You think you can communicate with that thing, then why don't you just go out there and try. We'll pick up your body, if we ever find it."

"We are more intelligent than that. We don't have to be reduced to that level," yelled Ellis.

"Shit! That's always the excuse. We don't need to sink to that level. I'm talking about our survival."

Sladen finally stood up and faced the group. She waited until they fell silent and said, "There is no choice in the matter. The choice has been taken from us."

Price nodded and said, "When do we go after it?"

"As soon as we can get ready," said Sladen.

"And that's final," said Ellis. "No more discussion about it?"

"It's final," said Sladen.

CHAPTER
16

While most of the others rested, Price, along with Grant, took the cutting tool to the second level. Together they sketched a sword on one of the metal doors, and then Price, using the cutting tool, began to trace the drawing. There was a quiet hissing as the metal melted but he was able to punch out a rough sword. Using it as a pattern, he created two more. That done, he and Grant picked them up and returned quickly to the central core.

In the central core, Grant and Price worked to take the rough edges off and wrapped the hilts in tight strips of cloth torn from the couches. Then Price, using his cutting tool, worked to put an edge on each of the swords. He tapered the blades to points. Grant rubbed them against the rough stone of the asteroid where she could find it, putting a better edge on each of the blades.

After several hours they had three useful swords. They weren't the sharpest ever created, but with the weight of the metal behind them, they would be able to chop off an arm or leg or head.

Sladen saw the three swords on one of the couches. She

examined them and then looked at Price. "Have you thought about how you're going to do this?"

"I thought that we all would be handling it."

Sladen sat down on the couch and wrapped one hand around the hilt of a sword. She lifted slightly but didn't pick it up. To Price, she said, "I'm Navy. Grant and Hunter are Navy. You're Army."

"But my Army doesn't use swords anymore," said Price. "Haven't used them for a hundred years, even if you count the ceremonial swords."

"You made them."

Price laughed once. "Grant helped me make them. She knew enough to help sharpen them. I think this is another cooperative effort."

"Then let me put it this way. I don't have a clue about what I should be doing."

"Okay," said Price, "I get the picture." He rubbed a hand over his chin and wished, for the moment, that he could create a razor. "The thing to do is head right back into that other area, three of us, and look for the creature. When we find it, we kill it. That simple."

Coollege walked up slowly, one hand on her stomach. "I want to go with you."

"Sorry," said Sladen, "but I don't think that would be wise."

"Tree?"

"She's right, Emma. You don't want to open those wounds. If we find the creature, you won't be able to help us. You rest another day or so and you'll be ready to help us."

"I belong there, Tree. More than these others. I belong there with you."

Price shot her a glance. She was dangerously close to breaking her cover. He said, "At the moment you are in no shape to help us."

She sat down and fingered the hilt of a sword, and then let her fingers feel the edge and finally the point. "I'm very good with edged weapons."

"That's a strange talent for an astrophysicist," said Sladen.

"The advantage of a liberal arts education," said Coollege. "I needed six credits of physical education and I opted for fencing."

"This will not be the same as fencing," said Price.

"I know."

"I think that Sladen and Grant should be the others on this little team," said Price. "If you hadn't been injured, I'd take you along."

"I don't want to be left with no weapon."

"That I can fix in a matter of a few minutes. You'll have to put the edge on it, but I can get you a long knife or something."

Ellis walked over and looked down at the weapons. He picked one up, swung it to the right, and then dropped it back to the couch. "I hope you're happy," he said.

"Delighted," said Price. "You're lucky that you have someone like me to protect you since you aren't willing to do it."

"Don't do me any favors," said Ellis. "You're trying to protect yourself."

"Fuck you," said Price.

Sladen, trying to break up the coming fight, said, "When do we get started?"

"As soon as we can," Price said.

Sladen picked up one of the swords, stood flat-footed, holding it in front of her.

Price pushed Ellis out of the way. To Sladen, he said, "No, hold it like this. Keep the point between yourself and the creature. Up on the balls of your feet, ready to move. Your job is to protect yourself and distract the creature and I'll take care of the rest."

"Sure."

Price believed they would be safe until they entered the other compartment. He kept his eyes opened, but he pressed forward rapidly, Sladen behind him and Grant bringing up the rear.

Once through the door, they spread out slightly, moving slowly, searching carefully. They studied the floor, looking for signs of the creature. They checked the side rooms quickly and when they found nothing, moved on to the next.

They moved deeper, keeping to the right-hand channels. At first the floor and walls were black rock with light fixtures hung overhead. As they continued on, they reached a portion where the floors were smooth and the walls polished. The lights were brighter. It was almost a carbon copy of the area they had discovered when they entered the asteroid.

They burst out of the corridors and onto a balcony that made them think, for a moment, they had somehow reached their own central area. But then Price noticed that the computers had not been touched, the couches hadn't been ripped, and there were humans below them.

Sladen joined him at the rail. Lying on the floor, behind the couches, were fifteen or twenty bodies. She shot a glance at Price and said, "What the hell?"

"I don't know."

"Let's get down there," said Grant.

"Wait," said Price. He surveyed the area below but it looked as if it had been deserted for years. No sign of anything down there living and no sign that anything had moved.

"We take it slow. We know that we're not alone in this thing. Grant, you wait up here until I reach the bottom and signal you. Understand?"

"Yeah."

"Okay." Price ran a hand through his sweat-slicked hair. "We take it easy."

He walked to the stairs, crouched, and examined the floor below him. Satisfied that there was nothing hiding close, he began to descend. When he reached the bottom he walked out to where Grant could see him and waved up to her.

As she began down, following Sladen who had reached the halfway point on the stairs, Price knelt near one of the sprawled creatures.

It was dressed in some kind of spacesuit with a thick helmet with a faceplate that was frosted over. There was no way to call it humanoid because it had three legs. When the being stood the legs appeared to form a tripod. It hadn't been designed for speed.

Price rolled it onto its back and scrubbed at the faceplate with his hand. Two eyes on a rounded head stared up at him. No mouth was visible. He grabbed the helmet, twisted it, but it wouldn't come loose. He found a series of buttons recessed in the ring just under the faceplate and pushed them. He twisted the helmet again and lifted it free.

The face of the being was yellowish but the skin looked like leather and there was no real expression. He glanced at the gloved hands and saw only two fingers and two opposing thumbs. The arms were long and thin, as were the fingers.

"I wonder what happened to them?" said Sladen.

"I would think they didn't have someone who wanted to commit suicide with them. They stayed in their suits until their air was gone and then died. Suffocated."

"Except for this one," said Sladen.

Price stood and moved over. One of the bodies had been ripped open. The head seemed to be intact, but the truck was torn and one arm was missing. The suit and floor around it were stained a light green.

Looking to the left he saw another being that had been killed. There was no head and one arm had been ripped free. As Price checked the body he noticed something lying near the hand. "What's this?"

"Don't touch it!" shouted Grant.

"Why the hell not?"

"You don't know anything about it. Could be a weapon or a bomb. Maybe there are germs."

"It's a little late to be worrying about germs," said Sladen.

Price rocked back on his heels. "I think this answers another of our questions. I think it means that the builders of this thing are hostile."

"How can you say that?"

"We've been attacked and two of our people are missing. These beings were attacked. It only makes sense to believe that whoever or whatever built this thing is hostile."

"No!" shouted Grant. "I can't believe that. They provided us with everything we need to survive. Then they stalk us and slaughter us like sheep. It makes no sense."

"This is getting us nowhere," said Sladen.

Price ignored her and slowly surveyed the room. Had it not been for the bodies it would have been an exact duplicate of the one they had found. And if there were two, there were probably more. He could see nothing that suggested where the killer alien was hiding, or if it had been there recently.

"I think we should head back," said Sladen. "Let the others know what we've found."

Price nodded, not thinking about the impact of what they had learned. They had found another intelligent race. It seemed that several individuals from it had been trapped just as they had been. It opened all sorts of questions, but Price ignored them all. The only thing that he could think of was that they needed to report this to the others.

"We can't let our guard down," said Price. "There is one thing alive around here."

Grant retreated to the stairs but stopped there. She stared up, at the next level, her head bobbing as she tried to see if anything was up there.

Sladen stood near one of the bodies, looking down at it. "This is getting hairy."

"Very," said Price.

It almost caught them. Price had thought he saw something in the shadows but when he turned, it was gone. And then came the high-pitched scream that seemed to announce it. The creature leapt into the center of the tunnel, landing almost between Grant and Sladen. Sladen swung her sword up to chop down on the shoulder of the beast, but it smashed her in the face, driving her backward.

Grant spun but the alien's hand shot out, its claws digging

into her shoulder. She screamed and went limp, dropping to the floor.

Price sprinted back and hit the alien from behind, driving the point of his sword through its back. There was a sudden, loud shriek, like tires on dry concrete, and the creature whirled, jerking the sword from Price's hand.

It raked the air with its claws, but Price dodged back, ducking. He tried to grab his sword still sticking in the back of the creature. He leapt right and then left, but couldn't get a hand on it. He spotted Grant's sword, ducked and dived under the flailing arm of the creature. He snatched it up, rolled, and looked.

But the creature was no longer interested in him. Price's weapon had fallen from its back. It fled down the corridor, disappearing around a corner.

Holding his sword up, he yelled, "Come on. Let's kill it now."

He raced down the corridor, sliding to a halt at the corner. The alien stood about thirty feet in front of him, swaying. One hand was touching its belly as if looking for blood there. It glanced up at Price, took a step toward him, and raised its claws, ready to fight.

Slowly Price advanced, holding his sword in front of him, the point aimed at the creature's belly. He kept his eyes fixed on those of the beast. The face had a satanic look to it and the pointed ears were laid back as if it was about to pounce.

"Cover me," said Price, unaware that neither Sladen nor Grant was behind him.

He feinted forward, swung the sword, missed, and danced back, out of the way. The alien lunged, and Price dodged to the right, swinging the blade upward. He connected, but there was no force behind the blow. He barely cut the skin on the creature's arm.

The creature grabbed at the blade and caught. It grasped the blade in its hand, but Price jerked it free. Price thrust once, hit the creature low, but it fell back, retreating. Then, suddenly, it leapt forward before Price could react. It wrapped its arms around Price, trying to crush him.

For a moment Price tried to break the creature's grip, but couldn't do it. He suddenly went limp, as if he had been shot, and slipped down. He rolled clear and the beast turned to follow. Price came to one knee and swung his sword like a batter going for the fence. He hit the skinny leg and heard something snap loudly.

The beast roared in pain. It jumped away and Price leapt to his feet. Sladen appeared from nowhere, her sword in her hand, swinging it like a sickle. The beast retreated, its eyes dancing between Sladen and Price.

Price noticed that it didn't seem to be hurt, though blood was dripping from its back. It moved as if it could feel nothing at all.

It stopped in front of one of the doors, but rather than enter, it whirled to face him. Now the creature stood its ground, refusing to retreat.

Price attacked again, watched the creature dodge and then fake to the left. Price thrust once, as did Sladen, positioned to the side. One sword penetrated the creature on the side. Price shoved his weapon into the creature just below the face. He twisted his blade and jerked downward. The front of the beast opened up, green blood spilling and splashing to the floor.

As the creature fell to its knees, Price ripped his sword free, lifted it high over his head, and slammed the flat of the blade into the alien's skull, trying to crush it. There was a crackling of the bone sounding like a short string of firecrackers.

The alien collapsed to the floor. Price, his breath rasping in his throat, stood watching, his blade pointed at the creature. Sladen dropped her sword and then sat down, exhausted. She didn't look up at him and didn't look at the dead creature lying on the tunnel floor.

"You okay?" asked Price.

"Yes. Yes, I'm fine."

"Grant?"

"She should be okay. Cuts aren't too bad, though her shoulder is ripped up."

"Shit."

Price stood quietly, his eyes on the beast. When the blood stopped bubbling, Price used his sword to prod the being but there was no response. He kicked it once but it appeared the creature was dead.

Taking a deep breath, Price said, "That's got it." He lowered his sword, the point now touching the deck under his feet. He stepped to Sladen and reached down, helping her to stand.

"Are you all right?"

"I'm fine."

"We've got to get out of here," said Price.

"My sword."

Price picked it up and handed it to her. "Let's get Grant and get out of here."

He stopped suddenly and looked back at the room. The creature had seemed to defend it. He stepped over the body and glanced inside. There didn't seem to be anything of interest in it. Just a couple of small machines pushed back against the rear wall. Nothing to indicate that the room had been used as a lair by the beast.

For a moment he stood there thinking. They had found the creature and defeated it. If he glanced to the right, he would be able to see the body. He should have felt something other than exhaustion. There should have been some kind of emotional release, but he felt nothing.

Maybe it would come later. Maybe once they returned to the central core he would feel something more. Maybe they would all celebrate.

He turned then and with Sladen walked back to where Grant sat against the wall. Her flight suit was ripped and bloody at the shoulder. She grinned up at them weakly. "I think the bleeding's stopped. I don't think the wounds are very bad. They're not very deep."

Price picked up her sword and leaned against it. "How you feeling?"

"I'm okay. You kill it?"

"Yeah," said Price. "I . . . we killed it."

"You don't sound too enthused."

"You know," said Price, "Ellis was right. We find an alien life and the first thing we do is destroy it." He held up a hand. "We had no choice, but still."

Maybe that explained his feeling about it. There was no joy in having to kill an alien life-form that could easily be as intelligent as they were. No chance for communication or discussion. Just a fight until one of them was dead.

"Let's get out of here," said Sladen.

CHAPTER
17

They had no chance to get off the balcony. The instant they appeared, Barnes was on his feet yelling. "Did you find it? Did you kill it?"

"We killed it," said Price. "Give us a hand."

Ellis ran forward, starting up the steps. He reached up, almost as if to stop Grant if she fell, and then backed down the stairs. When they reached the main floor, he stepped closer and helped Grant to one of the couches.

Coollege, who had been watching, asked, "What in the hell happened?"

Sladen sat down and took a deep breath. "We found it and killed it."

Price said, "We found other bodies."

"De Anna and Jackson?" asked Ellis.

"No. Other aliens. Another group that appears to have been trapped as we were."

"What?" asked Hunter.

Price explained the situation. When he finished, Coollege said, "You think they were attacked too?"

Sladen stood and moved to Grant. She looked down and

then peeled away the torn area of the flight suit. The wounds had scabbed over and there was no sign of fresh bleeding. Sladen didn't like the looks of the wounds because they were punctures and not scratches, though they didn't appear to be deep. They could have been infected when the creature grabbed her. Grant's system would have to fight off any disease because they had no medicine. If the creature's claws were dirty, it could eventually kill Grant. Sladen said nothing about it. She just smiled at Grant and then sat down again.

"Seems obvious that they were attacked by something," said Price.

"Could the creature have entered with them? Something that followed them in?" asked Hunter.

"I wouldn't think so," said Price. "I mean, you need some form of spaceflight to get here. Even if it passed close to your home planet, you still need the capability to arrive here. There is no way that such a large creature could stow away without being spotted. It would have to have gotten here by itself at a different time."

"Are you sure the creature is dead?" asked Barnes once again.

"Yes," said Price. "I didn't listen for a heartbeat. Hell, I don't know if it had a heart, but it was dead. There was no question about that."

Ellis asked, "Did those other aliens have any tools with them?"

"What difference would that make?"

"Might give us something we don't already have. Help us get out of here."

Price looked at Sladen and said, "I didn't see any tools but that doesn't mean there weren't any there. We can go back to check some other time."

Ellis and Coollege kept questioning them for more than an hour. Barnes sat off to one side, listening, but saying nothing. He kept looking up, at the stairs, as if he expected the creature to reappear suddenly to rip them apart.

Sladen finally said, "We've told you everything we know.

Everything. I think it's time that we get some rest. It's been one hell of a day."

"We've got to explore that other section," said Coollege.

"I know that," snapped Price, "but we don't have to do it right this minute."

Ellis interrupted and said, "Say, I've been thinking. How do we know there was only one creature?"

From its control room in the center of the asteroid the maintenance man that had awakened when the computer program failed sat watching everything happening in the sample confinement areas on its monitors. It saw the humans break into another area. It witnessed them find the dead aliens and then the fight between the humans and the beast. It wondered why they were fighting and then it decided that it didn't want anything to do with either of the groups.

Finally it turned its attention away from the monitors. It left them on and recording so that it would miss nothing, but now it was tired. And lonely. That was the design flaw of the asteroid. It only contained enough room for a single maintenance technician. On long flights, there should have been two.

While the others rested, Hunter slipped away. She climbed the crystal staircase and stopped at the top to look back. No one had seen her leave. For a moment she thought about letting them know about her plan but then decided it didn't matter. The dangerous creature was dead.

She didn't hurry, feeling no pressure at all. She worked her way down the corridor, to the tunnel, and finally to the door that Price had burned the hole in. She stopped there, examined it closely, and then stepped through. She walked along the corridor and out onto the balcony overlooking the dead aliens.

She wasn't sure why she had come. She stood looking down at them, thinking that they held the clue that would allow escape. But then, they hadn't escaped. They had died still wearing their suits. She didn't know what she might learn from them.

Finally she walked to the stairs and descended. As she approached the closest body, she saw that it was just as Price had described it. It reminded her of a hot dog with a tripod. She tried to roll it over but it was too heavy for her.

Studying them, she noticed they all wore a belt covered with pouches. She tried to open one but couldn't make it work. She knew there was a trick to it, like the childproof aspirin bottles. Eventually she would be able to open it, but at the moment it was frustrating.

She saw one of the creatures lying on its back, or what she assumed to be its back because the faceplate was pointing upward. Through the cracked glass she could see two unblinking, staring eyes. Near the arm was some kind of patch or embroidery.

The patch was dull, mostly browns and blacks, which might be why no one else had seen it. The writing on it looked like someone had spilled paint on it. In the center was a strange symbol that looked like a cross between a pyramid and an oval. She tried to pull it free but couldn't.

Finally she stood up and took a quick look around. Tools and weapons were the things they needed most. But there was nothing she could find that suggested it would be of use to her or the team.

She spotted one of the creatures that had been attacked and walked over. At least the suits were open. She crouched near it and tried to find anything on the inside of the suit that would allow her to open the pouches, or that would be useful.

She leaned against one of the couches and sighed. She knew there were things she should be doing, but for some reason, her training had deserted her. Besides, there was nothing on the alien bodies that she recognized.

She turned and began to move from one body to the next. She looked up suddenly, feeling that she wasn't alone. She forced the thought from her mind, aware of the crawling sensation at the base of her spine.

She told herself that she was being childish as she moved forward. She found a creature that was slightly smaller than the others and her first thought was that it was female. Of course there was no natural law that said the female had to be smaller than the male, or that the aliens had to be divided into male and female.

But all that was just an attempt to fill her mind with noise because she was suddenly very frightened. She was sure that she was being watched by something. She knew that there was something behind her.

It was then that she saw the movement on the second level. She turned toward it and saw something standing there. It looked nothing like the creature she had seen in the tunnel or that the others had described. It was different, bigger, and for some reason she thought it was more deadly.

When she saw it, it began to move to the stairs. It began to descend slowly, its fearful yellow eyes staring at her, seeming to study her.

This thing was humanoid. It walked on two legs and had two long arms that ended in single, hooklike claws. The head was covered with black fur and it moved lightly, easily, almost like a dancer.

She smiled at it, holding a hand up in a typical Earthly manner. "Hello," she said.

She stood her ground as the creature came toward her. When it reached the main floor, she took a single step back. She wasn't scared, she told herself, because the thing facing her had to be intelligent. One intelligent creature had to recognize another.

The creature eased its way toward her, moving slowly, holding her with its eyes. She found that she couldn't look away, fascinated by it. When it lunged forward, jumping the last few feet, she was so surprised that she stood and screamed. The thought to run never crossed her mind.

The alien caught her with one of its hooked claws and held her fast.

•   •   •

Price awoke with a start, sat up suddenly, and looked around. There was no movement anywhere, just the quiet snoring of one of the others. He lay back and closed his eyes but then realized that he would not be able to sleep again. He was wide awake.

He sat up again, put his feet on the floor, and pushed himself erect. He rubbed his face briskly and wished there were a way to brush his teeth. They felt coated, as did his tongue. That was one of the things he missed the most. The ability to clean out his mouth and brush his teeth.

Then he noticed that they were one short. He raised his voice, "Hey! Has anyone seen Sara?"

Sladen sat up and blinked rapidly as if not fully conscious. "What?"

"Sara has disappeared," said Price.

Coollege stood. "What happened?"

"Sara's gone," said Price.

"Shit."

Sladen stood and brushed her hair out of her eyes with her fingers. "Okay, she had to wander off on her own otherwise we'd have heard something."

"You don't think she went to look at that other group, do you?" asked Coollege.

"How the hell would I know?"

"She's your friend."

Price interrupted. "We stick together from now on. No one leaves the main group."

"Now wait a minute," said Sladen.

"You have an objection?" asked Price.

"No."

Ellis who was sitting quietly said, "I'm staying here to finish my work."

"Everyone goes," said Sladen. "There are too few of us left now."

Barnes suddenly spoke. "I thought you said that you killed the alien."

"I did."

"Then where's Hunter, huh? What happened to Hunter?"

"She walked off," said Sladen.

"No, she didn't," said Barnes. "It came in here last night and carried her off just like it's going to carry us all off in the night."

Price turned and faced Barnes. "Why don't you just shut the fuck up right now. You've done nothing but complain since we got here."

"You are supposed to protect us."

"Now where in the hell did you get that idea?" asked Sladen. "Nowhere does it say that I or any other officer here is supposed to protect you."

"You're the soldiers. It's your job."

"I'm a sailor," said Sladen. "My job is to get you from one point to another."

"Then it's his job," said Barnes, pointing at Price. "He's a soldier. The Army is supposed to protect the civilians. It's their job."

"I'm an observer here," said Price. "Nothing more. I have been given no orders other than those of an observer. You have to take care of yourself."

Barnes looked to the others for support, but they avoided his eyes. He sat back on his couch and looked as if he were going to cry.

Sladen said, "Is there any reason for us not to try to find her now?"

"Breakfast," said Coollege.

"Carry it with you."

"You sure that you want everyone to go?" asked Ellis.

Sladen rubbed her face as if she was suddenly very tired. "Yes, all of us. No more loners, no more two-man groups. We all stay together until we have a few more answers. Period. End of discussion."

Price stood holding his sword in his hand. "I'm ready."

Barnes, looking at the weapon, said, "I thought you said you killed the thing."

"We did, but as long as we have them, why not take them."

Of course, Price was thinking about something that had been said by one of the others the day before. What if there were more than one.

Sladen, holding one of the weapons, started for the crystal stairs. "Follow me," she said.

Without another word, they climbed the stairs and headed down the corridor, toward the opening that Price had made. They kept the pace steady and figured that at some point they would meet Hunter on her return.

They passed the junction where the alien had been killed the day before. "Maybe we should check it out before we continue," said Coollege.

"Later," said Sladen.

They came to the other balcony and hurried to the railing on the second level. Sladen called, "Hey, Sara Jane, you down there?"

There was no answer.

They hurried down the stairs, reached the floor, and fanned out. Price headed off, trying to see if Hunter had gone down any of the lower corridors.

Sladen crouched near one of the bodies, as if it could tell her about what had happened. She glanced up and saw a very human-looking foot close to one of the couches. She felt her stomach turn over and was afraid that she was suddenly going to be sick. She moved forward and saw there was a human leg attached to the foot.

"Oh," she said quietly, and then again, louder, "Oh!"

Coollege saw Sladen turn pale. "What?"

Sladen pointed at the floor and then said, "I thought we'd killed it."

CHAPTER
18

To no one's surprise, the body of the alien was not where they had left it the day before. They approached the area carefully, afraid that there might be some trick, but there was none. Price was sure the creature was dead, the blood that had flowed from it had pooled on the floor and solidified. But the creature was gone. Or rather, the body was gone. And Price wasn't sure what that meant.

"It has to be dead," said Price. "It couldn't have survived its wounds."

"Then where is it?" asked Sladen.

"Crawled off to die," said Price. "Badly wounded, it crawled off to die."

Coollege crouched near the pool of blood but didn't touch it. "Maybe it can look like it's dead. Maybe it was just trying to end the attack."

"No, it's dead," said Price. "All we have to do is find the trail and follow it."

"That's unnecessary," said Sladen. "It's not going to be a danger to us again."

Coollege looked up and said, "Are you sure about that?"

"No," said Sladen. "But then, I did see it yesterday, after the fight. It looked dead to me."

"We've got to do something," said Ellis.

Price sat down on the floor and said, "We can make a couple of assumptions here. Obviously there is something else in here with us."

"Something deadly," said Sladen.

"What are we going to do now?" asked Barnes.

"We all stick together, period," said Sladen. "We don't panic. We get organized and we go out and find the alien and kill it."

"Or them," said Price.

"Or them," agreed Sladen.

"We don't know," said Ellis, "that there is more than one. We don't know if it is dead or not. At the moment, we don't know much of anything."

"None of that matters," said Price. "Our immediate priority is to protect ourselves."

Ellis said, "I may be out of line here, but it seems to me that a more productive avenue might be to try to escape from in here."

Price shook his head. "I'm afraid that won't work. We just don't know how to do it, and we'd have to be looking over our shoulder for this creature. No, we must hunt it down first, and then we can talk about getting out."

"Anyone have any other points?" Sladen waited and when no one spoke said, "That's it then. We go kill it."

The tiny band moved to its own side of the asteroid, watching the shadows and dark corners. They probed them all. They satisfied themselves that they were alone on their side and then expanded the search outward. They became more alert, trying to see through doors and into the rooms behind them. They were searching for spoor of the alien but they found nothing that could help them.

They moved quietly, Price in the lead and Sladen at the rear. The others filled in with Barnes right in the center where he had the best chance to escape if they were attacked.

Price poked at shadows with his sword, used it to pry doors upward, and pushed it around corners trying to spring any ambush that might be in front of them.

They walked down the center of the tunnels and corridors, searching for the enemy. Price felt that his head was on a swivel as he tried to see everything in front, beside, and behind him all at once.

Eventually they came out on the balcony again but avoided looking over the rail. No one wanted to see Hunter's body where they had left it. They were trying to ignore that for the moment. They also ignored the fact that Hunter's death suggested that both De Anna and Jackson were also dead.

Sladen felt her mood blacken. She wanted to chop up the central core, to smash the computers there, and to rip apart the couches. She wanted to destroy because that had been all that had been happening to them. Destruction. To break the thought, she asked, "What do we do now?"

"Systematically search this area until we're satisfied that the creature is gone, or until we find it and kill it."

"Right," said Coollege.

They worked their way through the second area and found nothing that interested them. No signs of De Anna or Jackson were found. No sign of the creature was found. All they knew was that Hunter was dead, killed by something that cut her apart, and they didn't know what it was.

They reached their own central area and found that nothing had been disturbed. They spread out, sat down, and ate in silence. Each knew that the danger wasn't over, but there was nothing they could do.

Barnes couldn't sit still. He stood up, walked around his couch, and then sat. A moment later he was on his feet, walking to the dismantled computer, looking at it, and returning. He sat again, took a bite of a biscuit, and then asked, "You get those things working?"

Ellis smiled at the question, happy to be back to something he understood. "The programming wasn't complete," he said. "That's the only thing that makes sense. It might give us a clue, it might help us, but there is so much that I have to learn first."

Barnes took a large bite from his biscuit, chewed, and then said, "Maybe that is what we should be doing."

"You can stay here tomorrow," said Price.

"*No!*" said Sladen. "We all stay together from now on. Too many people are dead."

Grant pointed up at the second balcony, saw a shadow that seemed to shimmer, and said, "What's that?"

"What?" asked Barnes. "Where?"

Grant stood and started toward the shadow. "I see something. Henry?"

Grant suddenly stopped moving, unsure of what she was seeing. It looked human, almost human, but it was lost in the shadows. Her voice now quiet, she again asked, "Henry?"

At that moment the thing in the shadow leapt. Grant stood flat-footed, unable to understand what she was seeing. Price understood it at once. Grabbing his weapon, he leapt forward, swinging. But then had to retreat as Barnes got in the way. The man stood without thinking.

The beast had one hand around Grant's ankle and was lifting her foot upward. She tottered on her other leg and finally fell, twisting around, putting her hands out. The creature started dragging her to the rear.

"Get out of the way," shouted Price, shoving Barnes to one side.

"Pull away from it," yelled Sladen.

Grant felt a scream bubbling in her throat, but she couldn't make a sound. She rolled to her back and kicked at the head of the alien. It released her as it turned to meet the threat from Price.

Ellis and Coollege moved, grabbing Grant, pulling her clear. Sladen and Price advanced on the creature, holding their swords up, ready to fight. Price swung at it and the beast ducked. The sword hit and bounced off.

The beast seemed unaffected by the blow. It danced away, a bizarre and wicked grin on its face. A greenish liquid ran from its hairline to its jaw. The features were almost human, unlike the thing they thought they had killed earlier.

Grant, with the help of Ellis and Coollege, scrambled across the floor leaving a trail of blood behind her. The creature had lost its interest in her and her friends. It was now watching Sladen and Price.

"We take it now," said Sladen.

The alien looked at her as she spoke. Then it began to turn slowly. First it looked at the scarlet trail left by Grant. It seemed to grin. It took a single step, its long arms, thick as beer barrels and covered with heavy black hair, hanging at its sides.

Price used his sword, swinging it from side to side. He hit the beast in the back, where the kidney would be if it had been human. It roared in sudden pain and spun, raking the empty air with its claws. It whirled, faced Price, and then attacked, driving him back. Price stumbled and fell, losing his sword as he went down.

Ellis jumped forward, screaming and waving his arms. He turned sideways, facing the creature with his hands up like a boxer. The beast came at him and he kicked at it, aiming at the crotch, but that didn't work.

The alien grabbed Ellis, wrapping him in a bear hug. Ellis twisted and Sladen yelled, attacking, but the creature slipped away, taking Ellis with it. Ellis tried a heel stomp that failed too.

Barnes could take it no longer. He screamed once and then ran for the crystal stairway. He scrambled up the steps, slipping and falling, and pulling himself up. He stopped on the second level long enough to glance back, and then fled.

The beast tightened its grip on Ellis. He wanted to shout for help, but he couldn't fill his lungs. He tried to twist his way free and felt pain flare in his back but didn't know what was happening.

Price was on his feet again, but wobbling. He held his

sword with the point down. Everything was blurring around him and he felt sick to his stomach.

The alien jammed its nails into Ellis's back. It pulled them free, dripping blood. The beast spun Ellis away, raking his shoulders and chest with its claws. As Ellis fell, the beast leapt on him, tearing at his stomach.

Price and Sladen advanced slowly, and watched as the beast took a single bite from the entrails. It then turned and leapt nearly thirty feet across the central core. It glanced back, grinned, and jumped up, grabbing the railing of the third level, hauling itself up. With a single, loud roar, it disappeared from sight.

Price sank to the floor. Grant sat at the side, trying to bandage her wounded ankle. Coollege took Price's sword, standing guard over him.

"We didn't do so well," said Coollege.

Looking at Ellis's body, Sladen said, "That is an understatement."

"Where's Barnes?"

"Ran."

"Shit."

Barnes was no longer thinking. He was just running. Running as fast as he could, away from the thing that was killing the others. He ignored the tightness in his chest. His lungs ached and his arms hurt, but he kept running, forgetting about everything except the scene in the central core. Finally he stumbled and fell heavily to the rough floor. He felt pain flare in his hip and side as the black rock cut into his flesh.

For several minutes he lay there, the only thing he was aware of was the pain. He gulped the air, tried to stop the burning in his lungs, and trying to find the strength to force himself to his feet.

Finally his fear of the alien got the best of him. He knew it was out there stalking him, and if he didn't move, it would find him and rip him apart. His only concern was to find a good place to hide until someone could find him and get him off the asteroid.

He pressed on, into territory that he had never seen. He passed a dozen doors and finally moved from the rough, black tunnels back into the refined and polished corridors. It was almost as if he had moved from one section of the ship to another.

He began looking into the rooms off the corridor, trying to find a place to hide. He was sure the alien had killed all the others and was searching for him. If he could find a good hiding place, the alien would never find him.

He came to a door and centered himself on it. The door responded, recessing itself into the ceiling. He stood there for a moment, looking at the dark interior, smelling something that was almost familiar. He stepped inside and the lights came on. He looked to the right and saw something that shook him to his very core. He stared at the thing that was hanging on the wall as an icy hand massaged his stomach and made his head spin. He thought he was going to faint and when he realized that he wasn't, he wished that he could.

CHAPTER
19

Stone stood at attention in front of the Admiral, his eyes focused on the bulkhead. He wasn't seeing any of that. He was seeing, in his mind, the blank surface of the asteroid as the team worked its way across the surface toward the outcropping. He was still wearing his lieutenant commander's uniform because he still wanted permission to return to the asteroid.

The Admiral said, "According to this, you have lost your ability to reason and it is recommended that you be relieved of your duties and placed on the retired list."

Stone nodded and tried to keep from smiling. It was no threat to him. While he might be placed on the retired list in his capacity as a shuttle pilot and lieutenant commander, he would revert to his permanent rank and to his former duties. However, to the Admiral, he said innocently, "Just what have I done?"

"I think that is fairly obvious." The Admiral spun the screen so that Stone could see that it was filled with information. "According to the four staff psychologists that examined you . . ."

"Excuse me for interrupting, Admiral, but I have been examined by no one."

"You are here to listen," snapped the Admiral. "I think it is time that you did just that."

"Yes, sir."

"These psychologists, who interviewed you individually as you talked to them in the club, mess hall, or in the course of your duties . . ."

Stone felt his blood begin to boil. He understood exactly what had happened now. No longer caring, he said, "You mean they spied on me . . ."

"Such interviewing technique, I'm told, is now preferred because they get the information at a level that is impossible under clinical circumstances."

"Spying."

"Whatever," said the Admiral, waving a hand to let Stone know that the discussion was over. "The point is, according to them, the loss of your crew is more than you can handle. Your insistence that they might still be alive is nothing more than a defense mechanism, but shows that you are unable to deal with reality. In other words, you cannot accept responsibility for the disaster so you've concocted this story so that you don't have to accept responsibility. By insisting on a return, which we refuse to authorize, you can now shift blame from yourself to the military and this command."

Stone rolled his eyes, stared upward, and said, "That's a load of bullshit so heavy that it is impossible for me to believe."

And then Stone knew what was going on. The Admiral was playing to an audience. They might not be sitting in the conference room with them, but later there would be a review of this. Tapes were being made. The Colonel had explained it to him. All he had to do was be clever enough to understand it. The Admiral was saving face by raking him over the coals. It didn't mean anything in the long run.

"Mr. Stone, I don't understand how you received a commission in the Navy. I don't understand how you ever were promoted to the grade you currently hold. I don't understand why you are not still an ensign in charge of the ship's stores. I will not tolerate that sort of language." Of course the Admiral knew that Stone had received no commission from the Navy. Stone had been planted on them.

Stone just shook his head. "Certainly, Admiral. Is there anything else?"

"I have a long list of things I want to talk about and if you have any hope of saving your career, I think that you'd better listen to everything I have to say." He grinned as he said it.

Stone just stood at attention and said quietly, "Yes, Admiral."

Slowly they worked their way from their side of the asteroid into the new territory. They moved along the corridors and tunnels, and checked every room they found, but there was no evidence that the alien had ever entered any of them. They found a lounge that looked just like the one on their side of the asteroid that included a painting of oranges and yellows and a tiny silver city seen through the mist. They found another food machine and then another tool room. But none of them showed any signs that the alien had been there or that it was interested in any of them.

And they continued the search for Barnes. They knew that he had fled before the creature had been chased away by them. Barnes had disappeared, but they were sure he would reappear. The creature hadn't been after him, so they weren't too worried about him.

After three or four hours of working their way through the tunnels, of terror that they would find the alien and fears that they wouldn't, Grant finally asked, "How much longer are we going to keep this up? We could search for years and never find any sign of it."

Sladen stopped, moving and said, "She's right."

"I know that," said Price. "But there's nothing else we can

do. Unless we set an ambush. We're not safe until we find it and kill it."

"And we could wait for years for it to stumble into the ambush."

"Then you've answered the question," replied Price. "All we can do is try to track it down."

"But if it knows how to open the doors and roam among all the sections."

Price stood still for a moment. "Then we make it come to us."

"And how do we do that?"

Price sat down, the point of his sword on the floor between his feet, and clasped the hilt. "It seems to be searching for us as we look for it. All we have to do is remain alert."

"And while we're doing that it will be stalking us."

"So that answers the question," said Price. "We can let it come to us. We're not dealing with a supernatural beast. It's something that can be injured and killed."

"How do you know?" asked Grant. "Just how do you know?"

"Because we drove it off once. We injured it badly. For Christ's sake, use your head."

"Then what we should do," said Sladen, "is return to our area, and wait for it to come to us."

"Not wait," said Price. "Prepare. Ambush it there and kill it there."

For nearly a full minute Barnes stared at the thing as if it were an apparition. He wasn't sure, at first, what it was, but when he began to recognize it, he felt his control slip. His arms were rigid and the heels of his hands drummed his thighs. He slipped to his knees and then curled into a tight ball as he whimpered, almost like a kitten that had been tortured for hours by a mean kid.

"No more," he sobbed. "No more."

The thing on the wall opened its eyes and couldn't see anything at first. Faintly, it heard the words Barnes spoke and tried to find him, but there was only a white lump on the floor.

The head was imprisoned in a wrapping of dark, tough material so that only the eyes could move. As it stared down, it thought it recognized the lump but the details refused to resolve themselves. The thing opened its mouth and croaked a single word. "Help."

Barnes jumped at the sound. He tried to force himself up but his muscles had turned to jelly. He could no longer move or speak or see. Images flashed through his mind that were blends of gray with splashes of color. There was no rational thought, just the blend of images that made no real sense. He was no longer thinking or feeling, merely existing.

"Help me."

Barnes might have heard the words, but he ignored them. He was sobbing uncontrollably, saying over and over, "This is too much. Too much."

"Help."

The single word transfixed him. He stared at the thing on the wall and pushed himself to his knees, away from the red and black specter that spoke to him.

He reached the wall on the other side of the room but didn't know it. He kept trying to push himself away, his hands, feet, and knees sliding on the smooth floor of the room. When he noticed that he wasn't moving, he looked left and right but there was no escape.

"Please."

Vaguely the images began to filter through the fog of his brain. The thing was humanoid. The arms and hands were held high, attached to the wall. The legs were spread, the black fiber crisscrossed up to end just below the crotch. Centered where the stomach should have been was a large white mass that pulsated slowly. Tubes and wires ran from it, connected to a machine that was shoved up against the wall.

All that Barnes could think of was the wasp that stunned spiders to feed its young. The living spider was caught and put in the nest until the young hatched. It gave the young something to eat until they were ready to punch out of the nest, into the world.

He focused his attention on the head and realized that it wasn't humanoid but human. It was another human. It was someone he knew.

He stood up, his back against the wall. He could feel his own stomach twisting and turning and tried not to be sick. He fought for control, but the room was spinning, the lights flashing. Finally a single word burst from his lips. "Jackson," he screamed. "Jackson."

"Help me," said Jackson.

"Oh, my God! Oh, no. My God! No!"

"Help me."

Barnes couldn't take it. He whirled, stumbled along the wall, unable to see it. He reached the door and banged on it, trying to break through it even as it raised upward. The instant he saw an opening, he dived through, out into the tunnel. He leapt to his feet and began to run again, back the way he had come, the sobs escaping from him in time to the pounding of his feet. He was screaming, but the words made no sense. Barnes was incapable of rational thought.

The remainder of the team worked their way from one area into the next, heading back to their central core area. They were spread out, watching the side tunnels, the rooms, and the shadows, searching for the alien.

Then, from a side corridor, came a quiet sobbing. Price looked up it and said, "Barnes?"

"Down that way, isn't it?" asked Sladen.

"The perfect trap," said Price.

"I'm not crazy about this," said Grant.

"Are you suggesting that we don't investigate?" asked Sladen.

"Of course not."

"This could be it," said Price. He rubbed his chin. "The alien might have shown itself."

"I'm not crazy about this," repeated Grant.

"We're wasting time. I'll take the lead. Liz, you've got the rear. We support one another and we move carefully."

"Let's just get it done," said Sladen.

Price took a step forward and tried to see to the end of the corridor. He thought he could hear the sobbing at a distance, but wasn't sure, the sound was so quiet. It could be a trick of the acoustics in the passage. When he moved into it, the lights came on close to him but they didn't chase all the gloom.

Price advanced slowly, his sword gripped in his hand so tightly that his fingers began to ache. He switched hands, flexed his fingers, and continued to move. As he got deeper into the tunnel, he heard another sound, like feet scraping on the surface.

"Someone's coming," said Coollege.

A second later Barnes appeared. He was stumbling along, his hands out in front of him as if he'd gone suddenly blind. Then he spotted the others and began to run again, crying almost hysterically as he did.

When Barnes reached them, Price grabbed him and stopped him, but Barnes couldn't speak, couldn't form the words. Price slapped him once, twice, rocking him, and then said, "What in the hell happened?"

"It's going to kill us all. Kill us and feed us to its young."

"What in the hell is he talking about?"

"I found Jackson . . ."

"Where?"

"Is he okay?"

"Is he hurt?"

But Barnes ignored the questions. He slipped to the floor and shook his head slowly. "He talked to me."

"Where the hell is he?" asked Price.

Barnes pointed back up the tunnel but didn't speak.

Price pulled Barnes to his feet and said, "Take us to him right now."

"No. I can't."

Price pushed Barnes and said, "You'll lead the way now."

But Barnes just collapsed to the tunnel floor and refused to move. "No."

Price crouched in front of him and slapped him as hard as he could. It sounded like a pistol shot, but Barnes refused to respond. He closed his eyes and shook his head.

"If we don't stay together," said Price, "it'll kill us one at a time. The only way we'll survive is if we all stick together. Now get to your feet."

Barnes looked up, the hate etched on his face, but he did get to his feet. He took a deep breath and in a very shaky voice said, "It's not far."

CHAPTER
20

It didn't take them long to get back to the room where Barnes had tried to hide. When they approached, Barnes stopped short and pointed at the door. In a quiet voice he said, "In there."

Sladen looked at Price and asked, "How are we going to handle this?"

"Just like we didn't know what Barnes had said. In other words, we're going to be very careful."

With Sladen clutching her sword and standing to one side, Price centered himself and watched as the door opened. When it was only partially up, he dived through and rolled out of sight. He came up facing the thing that Jackson had become. Just for an instant he thought he was going to be sick.

A second later the door opened again and Sladen was standing there. She looked from Price to Jackson and then back again. She felt her head spin and reached out for support. In a voice drained of emotion she asked, "Is he still alive?"

To answer the question, Jackson said, "Help me."

Sladen stood staring at the wall. She wanted to believe, with all her heart, that Jackson was dead, and had been since he disappeared because she didn't want to think about the torture. Torture that hadn't finished. But she had already heard him speak and knew the truth.

She moved closer and asked, "Frank, can you hear me?"

"Yes."

"Okay," she said, staring into his eyes. She wanted to run, wanted to get out, but couldn't leave him alone. "Okay. We'll get you out of here."

"Hurry."

Sladen glanced to the right, looked at Price, and asked, "Now what?"

"Cut him free and see if we can detach that thing from his belly."

"And if we can't?" she asked under her breath.

Price leaned very close to her ear so that only she could hear, and said, "Then we kill him."

Sladen stared into Jackson's eyes and asked, "What happened, Frank?"

There was no response, but the answer was obvious. He had been taken, captured, and was being used as a host for the young. There was no other explanation.

"It's not intelligent like us," whispered Jackson. The words came slowly, with great effort. "It doesn't recognize other intelligence."

Price asked, "Did it build this ship?"

"No."

"Where is it from?" asked Grant.

Price didn't expect an answer, but Jackson said, "From a star near galactic center."

"How do you know that?"

"It is teaching the young . . . I learn from that."

"What does it want?"

"To raise its young."

Sladen whispered to Price, "What'll we do?"

Price took a step back and looked at Jackson. It would

be no trouble to cut the webbing that attached him to the wall. The tubes dripping blood and the wires hooked into the machine were something else. Price didn't have the medical knowledge to know how to deal with those. And he didn't know if the white mass on the belly was hooked into Jackson. Maybe they could just slice it away, but maybe it would require surgery to remove it. If that was the case, then they could do nothing for Jackson except kill him.

Grant asked, "Where's De Anna?"

"Behind the machine."

Sladen said, "I'll get him." She grabbed the corner of the machine and pulled on it, sliding it around, out of the way. She twisted around, braced herself against the wall, and pushed. She saw an arm drop and turned so that she could see better.

"Oh, Christ!" she said, trying to get out of the way.

Price stepped over and saw that De Anna had been fastened to the wall upside down. His throat had been cut and his blood was draining into a long tube that looped over and entered Jackson near the right kidney. Two tubes from the food machine were hooked into De Anna. It looked as if he was being used to manufacture blood to keep Jackson thriving until the young could be born.

Sladen had moved forward again. "Is he alive?"

"Barely," said Price. "We remove those tubes and he'll die immediately."

"Don't kill him," said Jackson. "Please don't kill him."

Price set his sword on the floor and rubbed his face with both hands. He studied De Anna for a moment and then retreated a couple of steps. He could think of nothing.

"We've got to do something quickly," said Sladen.

Price bent and picked up his sword. He then moved around so that he was standing directly in front of Jackson. He touched the white mass, which he'd thought was soft and yielding, and discovered it was hard and cold. He crouched to look up at it but there was no gap between the edge of the mass and the skin of Jackson's belly.

With the sword, he tried to pry it loose, hoping to slip the blade under the white and pop it loose. When he couldn't lever it in, he tried to cut it. Jackson howled in sudden pain.

"Now what?" asked Sladen.

Price placed the point of his sword against the top of the mass and pressed on it, slowly building up pressure. But Jackson screamed again and Price stopped.

Price shook his head. "Maybe the cutting tool will work."

"What about Jackson?"

Price lowered his voice and said, "I don't think that Jackson is going to survive this."

Coollege leaned close and whispered, "Then we'll lose a valuable source of information about the creature."

"She's right," said Grant.

"What could you possibly want to know about that thing you don't already know?" asked Sladen.

"How to kill it."

"Use the cutting tool," said Sladen.

But Price hesitated. There were a hundred questions that had popped into his mind. As an intelligence officer, he didn't want to give up a source of solid information until he had learned all that he could from it. They would never have a better opportunity.

"Please," said Jackson. "Do something."

Price handed his sword to Coollege and pulled the cutting tool from a pocket of his tattered flight suit. He looked at Jackson and said, "I'm going to try to cut through the top of this carefully."

He pressed the cutting tool against the white mass. For a moment nothing happened and then a glow began to form around the blade. And suddenly Jackson began to scream in pain.

Price stopped cutting. "What am I going to do?"

"Cut it off him," said Sladen.

"It's not going to be any too pleasant."

"Just cut it off him," said Sladen.

Price pressed the edge of the tool against the mass and

held it there. The glow began again and Jackson screamed louder as the tool penetrated deeper. His voice cracked as he shrieked but Price didn't waver. He held the tool in place, sliding it downward, trying to open an incision in the middle of the mass, trying not to hear the screams. Jackson kept shrieking until he was hoarse and then suddenly stopped as he lost consciousness.

Price felt sweat bead and drip. Now that Jackson was unconscious, it was easier. He finished the cut and turned the tool but the mass cracked wide open. A cascade of blood and gore splashed to the floor. A large bloody mass fell free, trailing ropelike tubes behind it. They were attached to Jackson and his vital organs.

Sladen moved suddenly, swinging her sword, and with one swipe cut them free. Blood poured from all of them, pooling on the floor.

"Oh, Christ," said Grant. "Oh, sweet Jesus."

"I think he's dead," said Sladen, hoping the horror was now over. She'd been watching Jackson's face and wasn't sure that he had been sane during the last few moments.

The webbing pinning Jackson to the wall was beginning to disintegrate. Jackson's head slumped forward, his arms fell free, and then he slid down the wall into the pool of his and De Anna's blood.

A noise burst from the tangle of tissue on the floor. Something moved from the mass and through the blood. It was a small thing, no more than a foot across that looked liked a slug with eight or ten tiny arms around it. It lifted itself up on four spindly legs. Price tried to grab it and felt something razor sharp slice into the flesh of his hand.

"Grab it!" said Sladen.

"No," said Price. "Kill it." He raised his sword over his head to slam the point through the center of the small alien body.

The little beast began to shimmer. The arms and legs began to disappear, sucked into the body that began to elongate and segment.

Price realized what it was doing as the segments defined themselves. It was trying to assume the shape of a human baby because it believed that no one would kill a human baby. Price closed his eyes and jammed the sword downward, pinning the beast to the floor like it was a bug in a specimen tray. There was a single howl reminiscent of that made by Jackson.

Sladen attacked it with her own weapon, chopping at it. She hacked it into small pieces and then kicked the pieces apart so that they could not come together again.

Coollege stepped around the mess, to the back of the machine where De Anna hung. She grabbed the tubes that ran into his throat and jerked them free. His eyes sprang open and she was sure there was a moment of rational thought before he died. His eyes rolled back into his head.

Sladen fell, exhausted. She sat up, leaning back against the wall, away from the blood they had splattered. She looked at Jackson's body and felt as drained as she had ever been. Her head spun and her stomach was palpitating. She turned her head and threw up suddenly. She leaned over, got to her knees, and vomited again and again until her stomach was empty and she felt like she was being turned inside out.

Price knelt beside her and then gently lifted her to her feet. "Get out into the corridor."

She looked at him and then nodded, stumbling through the door.

Coollege looked at the mess and said, "Should we try to take some samples?"

"How?" asked Price. "For what or whom?"

She shrugged.

Grant asked, "Shouldn't we do something for Frank and Tom?"

"What?" asked Price. "We can't bury them and we can't cremate them. Our choices are limited."

"What are we going to do now?"

Price said, "I think that we return to the central core area and think about that."

"What about the alien?"

Price looked at the gore and the bodies. "It's going to be looking for us now. It's going to want to do this again because it failed the first time."

"Oh, Jesus," said Grant.

CHAPTER
21

In the cockpit of the asteroid, the creature that served as the maintenance man was trying to figure out what had happened. It had been watching the monitors and knew that the samples from one confinement area had contaminated those of another. Now it seemed that they were killing each other. That wasn't supposed to happen. The samples were supposed to stay separated, they were to use the various rooms that would help scientists gauge the intelligence of the beings, and they were then supposed to be examined and preserved. They were not supposed to break into other areas and destroy each other before the various tests could be finished.

It sat for a moment, stroking the fur of its lower arm. It touched a series of buttons near it and surveyed each of the confinement areas. It was surprised to learn that there had been several penetrations by aliens while it slept.

Using its computer system, it reviewed a number of tapes and learned that the one beast had gotten free and attacked a number of different samples. He found it interesting that one creature had lived so long.

Of course, there was nothing he could do about it. His job was to repair any equipment that had broken down to make sure that the flow of information never stopped. If the various samples were contaminating one another and killing one another that didn't matter, as long as the information was broadcast toward its home world.

It could always enter one of the areas, if it wanted. At the moment the last thing he wanted was to enter any area. He would stay put and continue to monitor. Maybe the situation would resolve itself.

Price had decided that there were too many avenues of attack in the central core. It would take all of them to guard it sufficiently. They moved to the lounge where there was room to maneuver, if they needed it, and there was a single door that led into it. If an attack came, which Price doubted since they moved there, they would only have to worry about a single point of entry.

One of them stayed awake and alert all night while the others tried to sleep. Price found it difficult. The images of Jackson and De Anna played through his mind. He couldn't imagine the horror of hanging on the wall while an alien embryo was fastened to his belly. Jackson had to know that he was lost in the asteroid and that no one would find him. He had to know that the alien would do everything possible to protect its young. A minute would have been like a year and an hour would have been an eternity.

Price tried to force the image from his mind. He tried to think of something else, anything else, but it wasn't working. There was no way to divert his attention except to review the injuries to those who were still alive. Fortunately for them none of those injuries were serious and all were healing well. Coollege no long felt any pain and Sladen insisted that she couldn't feel a thing. Grant refused to let anyone help her, saying that she felt fine.

But Price knew that they were lying, trying to stay in the game despite their injuries. Of course, unlike a game, if they were taken out and the remaining players lost, time could become lonely. A loss in this game meant that others were going to die, and that took him right back to Jackson hanging on the wall. He shivered once, feeling sick to his stomach.

Coollege sat down next to him then and leaned very close. When Price looked at her, she said, "I can't take much more of this."

Price rolled to his side and reached out, taking her hand. He studied her eyes; they looked haunted. Her face was white and she squeezed his hand tightly.

"I don't want to end up like Jackson."

"Neither do I, but I don't think it's going to happen. We know too much."

"What's that mean?"

"It got Jackson and De Anna when they were alone. It took them before we knew there was any danger. We weren't alert then. Now we are. We've armed ourselves. The advantages are now all ours."

Coollege slipped closer to him, taking comfort in the proximity of his body. She put a hand on his knee. "There is one thing that has gotten lost in all this. When the creature is dead, we're still stuck in here."

"Stuck but alive," said Price. "We've had to deal with this creature because of the situation, but when that problem is solved, then we can think about the other."

"What do you think they're doing on the ships?"

Price thought that he knew, but he wasn't about to say that. Instead, he said, "They're going to believe we died in the first four or five hours. There will be no attempted rescue." Before she could speak, he added, "But! They are going to want to know what happened. There will be another mission to the asteroid. No reason for them not to come, eventually. All we have to do is survive until they get here."

"All," said Coollege. That one word showed the enormity of the task they faced. All they had to do was survive until the fleet got around to coming for them.

"We need to get some rest," said Price.

"Why?"

"Because we are going to have a rough time tomorrow. A very rough time."

Coollege slipped closer to him and then stretched out. She continued to hold on to his hand. She wasn't going to let him get away from her.

Price looked at Sladen who had the next two-hour watch. She was sitting off to the side of the door, where she would be invisible to anyone or anything that opened it. She nodded at him and then smiled.

When they were rested and ready, and after they had eaten, they left the lounge and returned to the central core. Ellis's body lay where it had fallen, the blood around it drying and sticky. Nothing had changed. If the creature had returned, it touched nothing.

"Is there anything we should do here?" asked Barnes.

"I don't know what it would be," said Price.

"Our EVA suits," suggested Grant.

Price walked over and looked at them. The alien had not touched them. No one had touched them. They were safe right where they were.

"Let's leave them here. They won't do us any good in the near future anyway."

They left the central core and climbed to the third level. They walked down the finished corridor and entered into the rough tunnels where the alien liked to hunt. They circulated through the tunnels, found nothing, and decided to return to the room the alien used for its young.

They returned to the center, descended to the second level, and walked down the corridors. The closer they got, the more cautious they became. As they entered the last few hundred yards, they began to move slowly and speak in whispers. Price was sure that they would find the alien soon.

But the room was empty and looked untouched. The bodies of Jackson and De Anna lay where they had fallen. The scattered remains of the young creature hadn't been touched. That meant nothing by itself.

"Maybe we should just wait right here," said Sladen.

"For how long?" asked Coollege.

Aware that the worst tactic of the duck hunter was to move the blind trying to catch the ducks rather than letting them come to the blind, she said, "I want to keep moving."

"It'll come back," said Grant.

"Those on defense are always at a disadvantage. We sit down and we take on the defensive mentality. I think we need to keep moving."

"Then we should rest for a few minutes," said Sladen.

"A rest is good," said Price. "But we don't bunch up. We keep it spread out. We give that thing nothing."

Grant started to speak and then merely pointed. At the far end of the tunnel stood the alien. It stood there like a giant humanoid with two tree-trunk arms. It started forward, moving on short, powerful legs.

"What'll we do?" asked Sladen.

Price was on his feet, sword held out in front of him. "Spread out. Liz, you on one side of the tunnel; Emma, you on the other."

"Me?" asked Grant.

"Bring up the rear," said Price. "Your ankle might still be a little weak."

"It hasn't bothered me."

Barnes retreated until his back was against the tunnel wall. He remained quiet hoping to be overlooked by both Price and the alien.

Price nodded but kept his eyes on the creature. "We let it come to us."

The alien didn't move at first. It stood solidly, as if daring the humans to attack it but when that failed, it began a slow advance. It swiveled its head, as if watching everything around it, but the eyes seemed to be locked on the humans. It finally stopped ten yards from Price.

Without a word, Sladen attacked from the side. When the

alien spun to meet the threat, Coollege moved in, swinging her sword. It raised a clawed hand, missed Sladen, and whirled to meet Coollege. Price attacked and his sword cut into it. It reacted suddenly, prancing to the rear, opening its mouth, showing long, curved teeth. It held its claws up like weapons, trying to protect itself.

Coollege danced in, timing her attack, but the alien had figured it out. As she attacked, the creature spun to face her. One of the hands lashed out and hit the flat of her blade, nearly ripping it from her grasp. She staggered to the right but didn't fall.

Price shouted to draw its attention and then swung with his sword, connecting again. Blood spurted on the arm, drenching the fur.

Now the alien tried to grab his sword. Price faded to the rear while Sladen attacked. The point of her weapon cut into the back of the beast, but the wound was shallow, unimportant, no more than a scratch. As it leapt forward, away from Sladen, Price attacked again, but the beast was able to avoid the weapon's edge.

Seeing the first opening for her, Grant moved in and thrust at the creature. It seemed to ignore her, as it concentrated its attack on Price, who was busy staying out of reach. He ducked under the alien's arm and retreated.

With its quarry out of reach, it spun suddenly on Grant. She thrust with the sword to keep it away from her, but missed and it stepped closer, grabbing her arm. She felt white-hot pain flare as its sharp fingers cut into her flesh.

She tried to jerk her arm free but the creature wouldn't release her. She pushed then, hoping to drive the point of the sword into the chest of the alien, but that trick failed. The creature felt the shift of her weight and as she thrust, it jerked her close. It reached with its other hand and raked her chest with its claws. She felt the deep, flaring pain and dropped her sword as the world around her turned bright red. She screamed as the alien jammed its claws into her like so many knives. She tried to fall away, slip from its grasp, and dropped to the floor as it released her.

As she fell, it used both sets of claws again. It cut through the flesh of her stomach and thighs. She fell to her back and tried to escape but felt herself getting weaker and dizzier. She failed to realize that her blood was pumping onto the floor.

No one could do a thing to help her. Price tried to chop one of the arms from the beast, but the blade slid off, almost as if the flesh were armored. Grant's blood spurted in a red fountain, but the spray was getting smaller. Sladen tried to drag her clear as her heart beat a final time and Grant died from massive blood loss.

Sladen, now nearly insane with rage, leapt forward, swinging her sword with all her might. The alien ducked under the blow, but as it reached out to grab her, Price snapped his sword downward, severing the hand. It roared in frustration and whirled.

Price sensed the kill and charged in until he felt his blade penetrate the trunk. It spun to the left, grabbed the sword in its remaining hand, and jerked the sword away from Price.

Sladen moved in again, chopping. She hit it in the shoulder, upper arm, and then the chest. She missed it twice and then caught it in the side. Her eyes were nearly shut. She pressed the attack, forcing the alien to retreat.

Barnes, believing the alien was dying, dived around and snatched the weapon Grant had dropped. He jumped in, swinging the sword like he were clearing vines from a jungle trail. He missed once because the creature had fallen to its knees.

But Barnes misjudged it. He attacked again but got too close. The creature lashed out with the finger knives, revealing Barnes's throat and severing his jugular. He dropped the sword and grabbed his neck, blood pouring between his fingers. Barnes fell forward and died.

Now the creature's body began to shimmer and the sword that had been caught in its chest fell free, clanking to the floor. The arms shriveled up and the trunk elongated, the change progressing so rapidly that Price could do nothing to kill the beast.

The many arms that had been on the young appeared on the adult. It lifted itself on four short, skinny legs and began to spin.

Price tried to attack it, but the razor-sharp claws on each of the arms gave it a defense like that of a rotating power lawn mower. Any attempt to move in, to attack it, would be met with a whirling, razor-sharp edge. He hit it a couple of times, but the wounds were nothing. It was spinning faster, moving up the tunnel, away from the humans. When he realized what it was doing, Price threw his sword at it, but the weapon bounced off the outer shell.

He ran forward and grabbed his sword and started to chase it, but stopped. Divide and conquer, that had been the philosophy from the very beginning. He slid to a halt and watched as it disappeared in the distance.

He ran back down the tunnel to the others. Sladen was kneeling near Grant. "Jo's dead."

Price ignored that for a moment. "We almost got it. We almost got it."

"Jo's dead."

Price looked at the body. Grant's face was white, the blood drained from it. He knew that he should say something but he couldn't think of the words. Grant was a friend who had died trying to kill the common enemy. But all Price could think of was that they nearly killed the creature. There would be time to mourn later, if he survived. But there was no time to mourn her now.

He turned his attention to Barnes. His blood had spread, covering the tunnel floor. Barnes hadn't been a good "soldier," but he had done his job. He had tried to help. There was nothing he could do for Barnes now except try to kill the alien.

He turned his attention to his living companions. "Either of you hurt?"

"I'm fine," said Coollege. She was standing to the side,

looking down at the body. She looked as if she had just played a rough half of football. She looked as if she was completely exhausted.

Sladen stood abruptly. "Now what do we do?" Her voice was filled with anger.

"Kill it," said Price. "There is nothing else for us to do now."

"Then let's go do it."

CHAPTER
22

"We stay away from the central core," said Sladen. "We stay away from the areas where it would expect to find us."

"We have to go back sometime," said Price.

"Not for a while. We can find everything we need on the other side."

"I thought we had it that time," said Coollege. "I was sure that we had it. If only we'd had a net, it might not have been able to escape."

"But we don't," said Sladen. "We don't have anything that we need."

"But we could make one," said Price. "Just like everything else . . . we could make one."

"How?" asked Sladen. "Out of what?"

Price took a deep breath and then said, "I'll admit that our options are rather limited. It has to be something strong enough and light enough for us to work with, yet something that we can cut to the lengths we need."

"Spacesuits fit the bill," said Coollege.

"No," said Sladen, "we'll need those."

"Not all of them," said Price. "We only need three of them. The rest are useless now."

Sladen smiled for the first time in hours. "So we have to go back to the central core."

"And then we hunt down the alien and kill it before it has the chance to do the same to us."

Ignoring Ellis's body, they moved back into the central core. Price pulled the spacesuits from the storage, leaving those for Sladen, Coollege, and himself untouched. They then spread away from the stairs, the tunnel entrances, and Ellis, so that they could work.

It wasn't that difficult to cut the suits into long strips, tie them together, and form a net. The material was slippery but held together. The net didn't have to withstand much, just enough to give them an advantage.

When it was finished, Price stood up and said, "Let's go find the thing."

Sladen was going to suggest that they eat something and rest, but she knew that she was just trying to put off the hunt. She wanted a delay, any delay, but knew that eventually she'd have to go out to confront the creature. Finally, she said, "How are we going to handle this?"

"Emma, you need to control the net. Liz and I will distract it. You toss the net over it and when it falls, we attack it, cutting it apart. We don't stop until we are sure that it is dead."

"I just throw it over the creature."

"When I signal," said Price. "Not until I signal."

Price suggested they begin the search at the point where they had last seen the alien. They would see if they could track it from that point to its lair, Price was sure that it had one. They entered the tunnel, fanned out across it, and moved deeper into the tunnel. As they rounded a corner, they saw the alien crouching over Grant's dead body. The creature had reverted to the humanoid form but the body was smaller, the arms thinner and shorter. It was poking at Grant as if it could raise her from the dead.

"What'll we do?" asked Sladen.

"Confront it and kill it," said Price. "Let's spread out. Emma, you stay about ten, twelve feet to the rear until we're ready to have the net thrown."

"Right."

They began the advance up the tunnel, but the alien didn't see them right away. It was busy with the body, and then almost as if someone or something had shouted a warning, it turned its head and looked at the humans. It began to shimmer and the shape seemed to fold in on itself until it was sluglike with a hard outer shell standing on four skinny legs. It was smaller than it had been.

"Here it comes," said Price as the creature started toward them. "We've got to kill it this time."

Sladen dropped the point of her sword so that it was nearly touching the floor. She held it away from her body to protect her legs from the razor-sharp sides of the arms sprouting from the alien.

Price followed her move. He kept his side pressed against the wall of the tunnel. He moved slowly, his eyes on the creature as it came toward them.

When it was only a few feet from them, it screeched in a high-pitched whine. It began a spin then, slowly at first, as if getting a feel for the coming conflict. As it reached full speed, it veered toward Sladen.

She countered the move with the blade of her sword, but the speed with which it was spinning caught her by surprise and the weapon was jerked from her hand. It went flying down the tunnel and there was no way that she could get to it.

The creature concentrated on her, edging closer as she retreated. She hit the tunnel wall and stopped. She was up on the balls of her feet, ready to spring clear.

Price attacked, hitting the solid back of the slug with the edge of his sword. It bounced off harmlessly. He hit it again and it changed the direction of its assault.

With the path now clear, Sladen sprinted past it and down the tunnel toward her sword. She grabbed it, but the blade was broken.

Price retreated now, up the tunnel toward Sladen. That left Coollege almost directly behind the alien. When it turned to follow, Price yelled, "Now! Hit it now!"

Coollege leapt forward, her arms outstretched. With a flip of her wrists, she threw the net out, over the back of the slug. It landed open and collapsed around it. The spinning of the alien dragged part of the net under it and its feet tangled in it. The creature fell to its side and then rolled to its belly so that the hard shell could protect it.

As soon as the motion stopped, Price jumped, landing directly on the creature's back. He chopped once with the sword but the shell was too hard. He tossed it away and snatched his cutting tool. He pressed it to the center of the alien's back, pushing with all his might.

The slug bucked, trying to throw him off. When that failed, it tried to stand, but couldn't do it. The struggling became more frantic and Price held on tightly. The creature began to scream, sounding like a turbine about to overspeed.

The shape began to change, long tentacles reaching for him, grabbing at this feet, legs, and arms. Price kicked and punched, trying to hold the cutting tool over the solid mass of the shell. He could see a glow around the tool but didn't know if it was from the tool or the creature.

There was a sudden stink, and a bubbling at the back of the slug. It gave a violent shrug and Price nearly fell off. He slipped to one side, dragging the cutting tool with him. The whole back of the beast exploded, erupting in a foul-smelling mass that splattered the walls and ceiling of the tunnel.

Price rolled free and leapt to his feet. He grabbed his sword and whirled. Coollege had fallen to the floor and covered her head as if she expected a cave-in. Sladen stood with her broken sword held at the ready.

The dying alien struggled a final time to its feet, took a

shaky step toward the room where its young had been, and collapsed again. There was a quiet mewing that finally faded as the bubbling from its back stopped.

Price used his sword, hacking at it as he had the young. He chopped until it broke in half and a bloody mass seeped out, onto the tunnel floor.

"Is it dead?"

"I don't know."

"What are you going to do?"

"The same thing that we did to the little one. I'm going to chop it into little tiny pieces." He began to hack at it, splintering pieces from the hard shell.

Sladen moved down the tunnel and helped Coollege to her feet. "You okay?"

"Fine. You?"

"I'm not hurt." She hitchhiked a thumb over her shoulder, toward Grant's body. "What do you think it was doing?"

"Probably looking for a new host," said Coollege.

Price had jammed his sword into the creature's back and was trying to pry the shell open. He then cut apart the flesh, kicking the pieces all over the tunnel floor.

"Do you have to do that?" asked Sladen.

"I don't know but I'm not going to take any chances. I'm going to make sure the damned thing is dead."

Coollege watched until Price had spread bits of the creature over the entire area. When he stopped hacking at it, she touched him on the shoulder. "Do you think this has ended the problem?"

He dropped his sword on the floor and embraced her. "I think this has stopped part of the nightmare. We have time now. We don't have to worry about something coming out of the dark to kill us."

Sladen said, "I don't feel much. I thought I would be singing and dancing but I feel nothing."

"It's the loss you feel," said Price. "So many of our friends gone because of this thing. That's beginning to sink in now."

"Let's get out of here," said Sladen.

Price released Coollege and took a final look around. It wasn't much of a battlefield, but it accounted for almost fifty percent of their lost and a hundred percent of the enemy's. In those terms, it had been a major fight.

CHAPTER
23

Stone stood in the shuttle bay and looked at the crew that was being assembled. This was not a scientific party that was going to study an object of a curious nature. This was a military landing team that was going in to learn what the hell had been happening.

The problem was that Stone would only be an observer, watching as the team prepared for launch. The Admiral had made it clear, and the Colonel had underlined the decision. Stone would not be allowed to go. Instead he spent days briefing the new crew and the landing team leader on what he'd seen on the asteroid.

Stone had begged for a chance to travel with the team but the answer had been no. He could help, they needed his help, but the makeup of the final team was already decided. That was it.

Jane Kristianson was next to Stone. She said, "Well, we're about to learn more about that asteroid."

"Looks like the Admiral didn't take your advice about staying away."

"Sometimes a hands-on approach is the only way to learn everything."

"If they don't get caught on the inside."

Kristianson laughed. "They have everything they need." She stopped talking for a moment and then said, "Say, shouldn't you be telling me that the soldiers will be able to get themselves out of any trouble. The last time it was the scientists who got into trouble."

"I'm just mad because I don't get to go. I was told that I would be going, but I guess those planning it felt that I could make no contribution." Stone knew what had happened. If the Admiral hadn't learned he was in the Army, he would have been on the shuttle. Politics reared its ugly head.

He continued, telling Kristianson, "They will be able to get themselves out of trouble. They're prepared for everything."

"That's more like it."

The Klaxon sounded, announcing the preparations for the launch of the shuttle.

"We'd better clear the shuttle bay," said Stone.

"Sure. You really wanted to go?"

They reached a hatch and it irised open. Stone stood back and gave the scientist a chance to exit. Stone followed and then said, "You going to the viewport?"

"No," said Kristianson. "I don't need to see that."

"Well I do," said Stone. If she had asked him to explain that, he couldn't have. Watching the shuttle slip out of the bay and into space. He wouldn't be able to see it as it dashed across space, or as it touched down on the asteroid. All he could do was listen to the radio communications and be prepared in case something else went wrong.

Kristianson said, "We'll have the answers soon."

"Yeah," said Stone. "That's what I'm afraid of."

"The key," said Sladen, "is the computer. We have a whole bank of them, and if we're going to get out of here, then the computers will provide us with the way."

"Sure," said Price. "We don't need a computer, we need a radio."

Coollege, who was sitting on one of the couches, eating

a biscuit, said, "There has to be a radio around here somewhere." She didn't even look up at the others. Just made the
announcement and kept eating.

"Why do you say that, Emma?" asked Price.

"Well, it figures, doesn't it? I mean, this ship doesn't travel
faster than light. The quickest way of providing data to the
builders is with the radio. Therefore, all we have to do is
find it."

"Now," said Price, "that is so simple that I'm surprised
that we didn't think of it before."

"It means," said Coollege, continuing, "that there must be
a cockpit area."

"Of course," said Price. It was so obvious that it was
natural.

"So we find that area and then use the radio equipment to
make our Mayday call," said Coollege.

Price felt relaxed. The major problem had been eliminated.
They were alone in the asteroid and all they had to do was
find the radio equipment. He knew that it was a long shot,
but after the pressure of the last few days, he couldn't get
upset. At the moment all he could think of was that they had
succeeded in surviving. They had won the battle.

The maintenance man, hidden in the center of the asteroid,
protected by metal walls and electronic webs, watched the
battle between the aliens. It didn't know which was the
aggressor and which were the defenders, but that didn't
matter. The information had been recorded and was being
transmitted toward the galactic center.

Another detector sounded and it turned slowly, toward one
of the outside monitors. Although the craft was still distant,
it could see that the ship was coming toward the asteroid.
That was a first. No one, according to the records it had
studied, had ever returned to the asteroid. Some had escaped,
returning to their homes, but none had ever been rescued.

Price sat cross-legged on a couch, staring at the computers

that ringed the core area. Bits and pieces were scattered on the floor, as were the tools that Ellis had used on them. Price had no clue about it, wondering if there wasn't something he could do with it.

"Well?" asked Coollege. "What have you figured out about this, Tree?"

"That I don't have the slightest idea of what Ellis was doing and how to finish it. This is far beyond me."

"Then we have to look for the radio," said Coollege. "It's the only solution. These computers were just more of the tests but Ellis was too caught up in the situation to see it."

Price knew that she was right but didn't want to admit it simply because it would mean that he had no more answers. All along, he'd had answers, but then the questions had been simple. Or before the questions could be formed, the questions were answered. It was a feeling that he didn't like. He wanted to be thought of as the man who knew everything.

"Or maybe we could build a radio out of the electronic components scattered around here."

Price twisted around and looked at Sladen. She was standing with her back to them, looking at the crystal stairs and the tunnel entrance beyond it. "Liz?"

She didn't turn. "What?"

"You know anything about radio?"

She ignored the question. "You hear something?"

Price was suddenly alert. He stood, glanced to where his sword was, and said, "No."

Sladen looked at Price and then pointed. "I thought I heard something back there."

"The alien?"

"No . . . something else. A pounding. I don't know."

Price picked up his sword and stepped closer to her. He studied the upper levels, searching for something up there.

"I think I heard it too," said Coollege.

"Spread out," said Price. "Let's be ready."

There was a burst of noise above them and a shape flashed near the railing on the third level. Price dropped to a knee, crouching behind one of the couches.

And then Sladen was on her feet, running toward the crystal stairs. She took them two at a time, slipping and grabbing the railing to steady herself. She was screaming, "We're down here. We're down here."

Price didn't understand it. "Liz! Stop!"

But she didn't stop. She kept running. She reached the third level and then slid to a halt. Price could see that she was holding her arms open, and then someone was with her. Not another creature but a human. Someone in a spacesuit carrying a rifle.

Price knew what had happened. Stone had come back. Troops had been sent. They had penetrated the asteroid and they had the ability and tools to get themselves out.

Coollege let out a whoop. She grabbed Price and kissed him. "It's over," she said.

EPILOGUE

The maintenance man watched the landing on the outside of the asteroid with interest. He saw a dozen or more creatures exit their ship, which then lifted off but stayed close to the asteroid. Those who remained behind entered one of the outcroppings and made their way deeper, until they came to the first of the doors. When it opened, they passed through and when it closed, they ignored it.

The maintenance man studied them as they worked their way through the tunnels, into the corridors, and finally out onto the balcony overlooking the core areas. He watched as the two groups, that which had been trapped for weeks, and that which had just landed, came together. It watched with great interest the celebration that followed.

Those alien creatures didn't stay long; they marched back up the corridors and tunnels until they reached the doors that blocked their paths. This time the doors didn't stop them for long. With everyone in a spacesuit, they didn't concern themselves with the vacuum on the other side. With explosives they had brought with them, they knocked it down and hurried into the outer chamber. Rather than letting the other doors be destroyed, the maintenance man touched a button to open them so that the creatures could escape.

Once they were outside, the ship returned, landed, and all the beings entered it. In moments it lifted off, turned, and disappeared from his monitors.

Now that the asteroid was empty again, now that there were no living beings in any of the sample confinement areas, the job of the maintenance man was finished. It could not repair the computers because the programming was incomplete. It could not remove the dead aliens because there was no place to store them. All it could do was make sure that the information was transmitted toward its home.

It made its report, saw that it would be broadcast automatically, and then changed course, ever so slightly. Satisfied with the results, it walked back to the sleep chamber, opened it, and climbed inside. With any luck at all, it would be home before being called on again.

The top of the chamber closed and it filled with a white gas. The maintenance man tried to see up through the gas but its eyes were too heavy. It closed them, thinking of home and the journey that still faced it.

It didn't know that its trip had lasted for more than fifteen thousand years, and that its home star had exploded a thousand years ago. It didn't know that the recall signal would never be issued because its home no longer existed.